or encourage electronic piracy of copyrighted materials. Your support of the author's rights is appreciated.

Please visit my website: www.degreenfield.com and sign up for my newsletter and get the latest news before the public.

I0571806

Every word I have written and published is from my noggin (brain, in case you don't know what noggin means). My fiction is all make-believe, from the deep dive into my wild imagination. All my nonfiction books have been researched until my brain has scrambled.

Nonfiction	
The Puppy Baby Book	Mastering Your Money (2022)
Puppy Adoption and Beyond	Writers Preparation Handbook
Mastering Your Money (2008)	What's Breaking Your Budget
Online Classes	
Writers Preparation Handbook	How to Format Word Docs Like A Pro
Cozy Mysteries	**Sci-Fi-Fantasy**
The Alcott Family Adventures	**The Thoi Series**
Hot Chocolate	Prophecy of Thoi
Bitter Chocolate	Gifts From Thoi
Spicy Chocolate	Love of Thoi
Nutty Chocolate	King of Thoi
Katz' Cat Series	Earth Calling Thoi
Katz' Cat	**Sci-Fi Romance Adventure**
Bill Hill's Pills	Forced Dreams
The Detectives	**Dystopian**
The Pact	The Last Dog
Discreet Conversations	Texmexzona
Books by my Alter Ego ~ DG Ireland	
Bonded Shapeshifter Billionaire Series	
Bonded	
Tothars	
Tilted	
Unforeseen	
Connected	
Need A Notebook?	
See my 54 themed notebooks on my website www.degreenfield.com/notebooks	
Screenplays formatted as books	
Plan B (Dark Comedy)	Where's Ralphie? (Family Comedy)
The God Child (Action Adventure)	Standing Dead (Drama/Tragedy)
The Far Corner (Sci-Fi/Psychological/Creatures)	Block Captain (Action Comedy)
Screenplays as TV Episodes	
Hot Chocolate ~ Episode 1	Prophecy of Thoi ~ Episode 1
Bonded ~ Episode 1	
See my screenplays and awards on my website: degreenfield.com Filmfreeway, ISA Network	

Plan B by Dawn Greenfield Ireland

Published by Artistic Origins

Copyright © 2022 by Dawn Greenfield Ireland

Book cover design by JewelDSign on Fiverr.com

Interior layout by Yours Truly (me)

ISBN:

• 9781940385501 eBook

• 9781940385518 Paperback

Dawn Greenfield Ireland

Artistic Origins

www.degreenfield.com

PLAN B

SCREENPLAY IN BOOK FORMAT

DAWN GREENFIELD IRELAND

ARTISTIC
ORIGINS

About Screenplays...

This is one of my screenplays that I have adapted into book format. The number of pages from script to book format changed due to the formatting characteristics of the publishing program to create eBooks and paperbacks.

In case you are not familiar with the elements of a script, I'll give you a boost so you enjoy reading these pages.

FADE IN: opens the screenplay.

INT. means any interior scene, such as a room, building, barn—anywhere inside.

EXT. means any exterior scene, such as outside on the grass, outside of the car, house — you get it, right?

When a character is first introduced, their name appears in all capital letters. After that, the name is displayed as normal.

Each character's action is in a separate paragraph.

Character dialog in a screenplay is tricky in this format. The character's name is in the center of the page, then the dialogue is inset at the left margin under the name.

I've done my best with the formatting, but it isn't perfect. You will notice that the dialogue and character names are centered.

FADE OUT. This is the end of the script.

If you have questions, suggestions, or tips, send me an email: dawn@degreenfield.com, but don't spam me.

FADE IN:

INT. HIGH SCHOOL HALLWAY - DAY

STUDENTS everywhere. Freaks, geeks, jocks, and the norm.

JUICE, 16, (real name Kevin), you can't miss him - neon-spiked hair on one side, shaved on the other, neon shades, earrings, and torn graffiti clothes.

He exits the bathroom in a hurry.

Juice glances over his shoulder.
Smoke billows out the bathroom door.

Alarms sound.

MR. REYNOLDS, 40's, rushes into the bathroom.

Reynolds exits the bathroom towing a GIRL, bound with duct tape, hair and clothes askew.

Both cough.

EXT. PRINCIPAL'S OFFICE - DAY

Juice sits outside Mr. Reynolds office on a bench, nodding to a silent beat. He fiddles with his slashed tennis shoes.

Mr. Reynolds - visible at his desk, through the mini-blinds.

BLOWPIPE, EDSEL and WORMIE round the corner and spot Juice on the bench.

> BLOWPIPE/EDSEL/WORMIE
> Ruh, ruh, ruh, ruh.

> JUICE
> Ruh, ruh, ruh, ruh!

Blowpipe's orange, short-spiked hair has a thin black tail half way down his back, ratlike. He's in a muscle shirt, black shiny bike shorts, and a black cape with red lining, over his clothes.

Blowpipe sports a diaper pin through one ear with assorted alligator clips attached in a chain. He tweaks his half mustache.

Edsel, at first glance, looks normal, dressed in black with his black hair slicked back.

The back of his head sports a skull tattoo.

Wormie - bald with no eyebrows wears burgundy lipstick. He's in a baggy shirt and rolled-up pants with sandals.

A MALE TEACHER, arm in a sling, has a black eye. He huffs down the hallway to Mr. Reynolds office.

> TEACHER
> (to the boys)
> You sound like a herd of pigs...

INT. MR. REYNOLDS OFFICE - DAY

Various award certificates adorn the walls, family pictures on the desk.

The teacher lets loose on Mr. Reynolds.

> TEACHER
> Kevin Undertosh...

Door slams. An argument is visible through the blinds.

Juice, Edsel, Wormie & Blowpipe watch through the mini-blinds with interest.

> JUICE
> Looks like someone's not going to
> win the popularity contest.

The boys screech with laughter.

EXT. STREETS - NIGHT

Blowpipe's junker car weaves down the road, a song blares on the radio.

Juice, Wormie, and Edsel hang out the windows. They laugh crazily.

The car jumps the curb, cuts across the median going the wrong direction.

Horns blast, cars evade.

The junker car u-turns. It weaves down the road and screeches to a halt in front of a video store.

TWO GIRLS, 15, faces masks of makeup, loiter in front of the store, texting and talking on cell phones.

Juice climbs out of the car through a window and stumbles up to the girls.

> JUICE
> Want to do me?

Music lowers.

> GIRL #1
> Fuck off!

The guys in the car snicker.

> JUICE
> That's the question!

> GIRL #2
> What part of "no" didn't you understand?

> JUICE
> Not in my vocabulary.

Juice grabs girl #2 in an embrace and plants a wet kiss on her lips. He releases her just as abruptly.

Girl #2 stumbles, dazed.

Juice climbs back into the car through a window.

The car screeches away from the curb as Juice wiggles inside all the way.

Girl #2 fans herself.

Girl #1 swats her in the arm.

> GIRL #2
> He kisses better than he looks.

Girl #2 gazes longingly after the car.

EXT. LUSCIOUS BACK YARD - NIGHT

The yard sports a gorgeous pool heavily landscaped, with muted lights. A paradise bathed in moonlight.

Juice tiptoes across the lawn clutching a bucket. He stands at the edge of the pool and dumps something into the pool.

He snickers.

> JUICE
> Hope you like my present, you bigoted,
> hypocritical rotten neighbor.

A security camera on the corner of the house sports a red light - recording.

Juice scampers back across the yard, vaults over the fence and disappears.

EXT. SWIMMING POOL - MORNING

A MAN and WOMAN, in robes, leisurely exit the house heading to the pool.

                    WOMAN
        What in the world is that terrible
                    smell?

They arrive at the pool's edge, then scream in rage.

Dead fish and crabs float on top of the water.

A cat sits at the edge of the pool and swats at a fish.

EXT. SWIMMING POOL - LATER

OFFICER LAJODA takes information from the couple.

A REPRESENTATIVE of the security company stands by.

                REPRESENTATIVE
            We'll email you the file.

EXT. STORE - DAY

Juice stands on a sidewalk, in plain sight, and sprays artistic
graffiti onto the exterior wall of a store.

A police car driving in the opposite direction makes a u-turn
and pulls to the curb.

Officer Lajoda gets out of the car and approaches Juice.

Juice, in a doped-up stupor, paints to his heart's content.

                OFFICER LAJODA
            Son, you better have been hired to

do that.

Juice, startled, turns, paint can in hand, still spraying.

Paint sprays across Officer Lajoda's chest.

Juice stands back and appraises the shirt.

> JUICE
> Cool. Think I'll come up with a
> product line for cops.

The STORE OWNER comes out of the store and joins the cop.

Officer Lajoda snatches the can from Juice, grabs him by the shirt collar and proceeds to the police car.

He deposits Juice in the back seat.

> OFFICER LAJODA
> I'm sure you're familiar with this
> view.

> STORE OWNER
> I'm pressing charges! I never want
> to see that kid again. He's nothing
> but trouble.

Officer Lajoda takes down information.

INT. POLICE CAR - DAY

Officer Lajoda drives.

> JUICE
> Dude, do the siren and lights.

Officer Lajoda glances at Juice in the rear view mirror.

> OFFICER LAJODA
> Fun time is over, kid.

Juice sulks.

INT. COURTROOM - DAY

The Store Owner, the Pool Owners and the Security Rep are among the courtroom mass.

The BAILIFF sits at a small table with a phone.

Juice sits at a table with an ATTORNEY.

His family sits on the bench directly in back of him.

FERN (Mother), 44, poodle-perm hair, starched white shirt, red scarf that compliments her navy suit, appears teary.

BERT (Father), 46, in his immaculate pin-striped suit, sits ramrod straight, mouth in a firm line showing his disillusion.

KIMMIE (7), cute and stylish, colors a picture.

KYLE (12), a definite heartthrob, watches a movie on his iPad.

EMILY (Grandma), 66, white hair perfectly coiffed, wears designer eyeglasses, and crochets furiously.

EARL (Grandpa), 67, in spotless, starched, coveralls and round, wire-rimmed eyeglasses, sends a kiss to Emily.

The JUDGE enters.

> BAILIFF
> All rise, the honorable James P.
> Thaddeus is present.

Everyone stands.

Judge Thaddeus sits.

> JUDGE
> Be seated. Let's proceed.

Everyone sits.

> BAILIFF
> The State vs. Kevin Undertosh.

The judge visibly shudders. He picks up a file, snaps it open, glances at the page, then at Juice.

Officer Lajoda enters and sits.

Juice waves to him.

The attorney elbow's Juice.

Juice sulks.

> JUDGE
> Kevin, I thought I told you the last
> time I saw you that if you were
> brought into my court again, I'd
> throw the book at you.

> JUICE
> We tried to get a different court,
> dude.

The attorney stands abruptly.

> ATTORNEY
> Your honor, my client is truly sorry
> for the occurrence and promises never
> to stray outside of the confines of
> the law again.

Juice's mouth drops open.

> JUICE
> When did I say that?

The judge grimaces.

> JUDGE
> Kevin, I'm placing you on probation
> for one year and I will keep your
> file on the corner of my desk.
> I promise to personally check with
> your probation officer for progress

reports.
(Beat)
And furthermore, I fine you $500.

The judge slams the gavel.

Fern jumps to her feet.

> FERN
> Please, your honor, can't you send
> him to prison?

The pool people jump to their feet.

> MAN
> What about my pool? I'm suing you,
> Undertosh.

Bert stands and tries to coax Fern back to the bench.

> BERT
> Fern... don't make matters worse.

Fern twists away from Bert.

> JUDGE
> I'm truly sorry, Mrs. Undertosh.

> FERN
> What about a detention center?

The store owner jumps up.

> STORE OWNER
> You're letting the scourge of society
> back on the streets? Who's going to
> protect us?

The judge bangs the gavel.

> JUDGE
> Order. Order in this court!

The family members stand and proceed toward the door.

Bert ushers Fern by the arm.

She struggles out of his grasp and faces the judge.

> FERN
> Boot camp? What about boot camp,
> your honor?

Bert guides Fern out of the courtroom door.

> FERN
> Can't you try him as an adult?

The judge lowers his head in sympathy.

INT. KITCHEN - DAY

SUPER: SIX MONTHS LATER

The Undertosh family sit at the kitchen table, breakfast in progress, one chair vacant.

There appears to be an undercurrent of nervousness.

Suddenly the kitchen door swings open and slams into the wall.

The family members flinch as Juice towers in the doorway.

Fern shoves her chair back and rushes to Juice.

FERN
Good morning, Kevin.

JUICE
Juice to you! I'm starving. What's
for breakfast?

FERN
Grandpa made pancakes and eggs, dear.

Juice approaches the table. He snatches a buttered pancake, dripping with syrup, from Kyle's plate.

KYLE
Hey!

He licks it. He makes a face and drops the pancake back on Kyle's plate.

KYLE
Mommm!

JUICE
What'd you put on this thing, dude?
(to Fern)
I want something else.

Fern goes to the refrigerator, grabs the handle but doesn't pull.

FERN
What could I get you, dear?

Juice shoves her out of the way.

Bert jumps up, throws his napkin down on the table and shakes a finger at Juice.

BERT
Don't you treat your mother that way.

Juice glares at Bert. He yanks the refrigerator door open and looks inside.

He picks up a carton of milk, smells it, then drops it on the floor.

Juice grabs a bowl of tuna salad, smells it, sticks his tongue in it, then drops the dish on the floor.

Next follow a couple of dishes and jars.

JUICE
Nothing to eat. Gimme money.

Earl and Bert rummage through their pockets and pull out bills.

Juice grabs the money.

Kyle jumps out of his chair.

KYLE
Can I go with you?

Juice glares at Kyle.

> JUICE
> Get lost.

Juice leaves.

O.S. the door slams.

Kyle sits in his chair. He rests his chin in his hands.

Fern cries.

> FERN
> I can't take it anymore. Call his
> probation officer and see if
> they'll put him in jail.

> BERT
> Hon, they're not going to do that.

> EARL
> Call the school and talk to his
> counselor. Maybe we can get
> him into a military school.

> BERT
> Worth a try.

Bert pulls out his phone, glances at a list on the wall and dials.

> BERT
>
> Ms. Morex? Bert Undertosh, Kevin's
> father.
> (Beat)

Juice? Yes. We're having problems...
what? Yes, I'm fine. I'd like to
make an appointment... what? Yes,
she's fine. Stays out all night, drugs... what?
Kicked the ladder? Fell on who?

Bert listens. Rubs his eyes.

INT. MS. MOREX' OFFICE - DAY

MS. MOREX, middle-aged with half-glasses, a bouffant hairdo and old, out of date clothes.

She sits at her paper-stacked desk and writes in a file.

Bert and Fern arrive. Bert knocks on the open door.

Ms. Morex jumps up and rushes to them. She shakes their hands hard, looks them over, amazed.

She leads them to chairs.

MS. MOREX
You look marvelous!

FERN
Why thank you. We just don't know
what to do with Kevin. He's turned
into such a monster.

MS. MOREX
He's missed a lot of school, and
gets into mischief when he's
here, but we figured it's because of the
accident.

> BERT
> Mischief? Accident?

Ms. Morex appears puzzled. She opens a folder and skims the contents.

> MS. MOREX
> We didn't call because we have a
> letter here stating that you were
> all killed in a plane crash over
> Mount Fuji when you were in Japan
> last year.

> FERN
> We've never been to Japan.

> BERT
> Doesn't someone verify something
> this serious?

> MS. MOREX
> It states here that Juice would be
> staying with his uncle over on Craig
> Street.

> BERT
> That's where Wormie lives.

All appear perplexed.

INT. SCHOOL CORRIDOR - DAY

Juice rough-houses with passing STUDENTS. He knocks books out of a NERD'S arms. Juice laughs uncontrollably.

BRENDA, a cute, fashionable 16-year old, steals a peek at him and shakes her head in disgust.

MS. MOREX' OFFICE - DAY

Juice enters, laughing. He appears momentarily stunned to see his parents across the desk from Ms. Morex.

> JUICE
> Yo! I'm here!

> MS. MOREX
> It appears your parents' bodies have
> been found.

An AIDE brings in another chair.

Juice picks up the chair and throws it at the Aide.

All scream.

EXT. JUNIOR HIGH/MIDDLE SCHOOL - DAY

Kyle exits the school amid the throng of STUDENTS.

FOUR GANG MEMBERS, pants low showing boxers, come up behind Kyle.

> BOY #1
> Hey, there's the freak's brother.

> BOY #2
> Where's your freak brother, kid?

> BOY #3

Oooh, I'll bet he's scared.

The boys walk past Kyle, bumping him and socking him while laughing.

> BOY #4
> (in high voice)
> Don't pick on me!

> BOY #1
> You gonna tell your freak brother?

Kyle walks with his head down.

INT. KITCHEN - NIGHT

Bert, Fern, Earl and Emily sit at the table in deep discussion. They nervously look at the swinging door.

> BERT
> The plan is, the school agrees to
> wait and see if this psychiatrist
> will help. If not, Kevin will be
> placed under an indefinite suspension.

> EMILY
> Great.

> EARL
> Let's hope the shrink works,
> otherwise, we're stuck with him full
> time.

All appear haggard.

INT. DR. ROBBELL'S OFFICE - DAY

A wall length planter of bamboo reaches to the ceiling. A hammock suspends from the ceiling, nearby.

A massive cherrywood desk at one end of the huge room. A bar sink with cabinets and counter top line a wall.

A group setting of two loudly printed love seats and a couple of straight back chairs complete the place.

DR. JONATHAN ROBBELL, 40, in a white karate outfit, sits on the floor in a yoga position, eyes closed, meditating.

A cellphone shrills beside him.

Dr. Robbell's eyes pop open and stare crazily.

The phone rings again.

He grabs the phone.

> DR. ROBBELL
> Yes?

> RECEPTIONIST (O.S.)
> Undertosh.

> DR. ROBBELL
> Send them in.

He gets up and stretches.

Bones creak.

Bert, Fern, and Juice enter.

Dr. Robbell does some karate moves, then shakes hands and introduces himself.

Bert and Fern's eyes open wide.

> DR. ROBBELL
> (to Juice)
> You must be Kevin.

> FERN
> Call him Juice.

> DR. ROBBELL
> Juice! Juice, Juice. The Juice
> of Kevin!

He grins at the family.

Juice appears bored.

Dr. Robbell nudges Juice.

> DR. ROBBELL
> That's your life force, you know.

Juice nudges Dr. Robbell much harder.

Dr. Robbell leads them over to the sofas.

> DR. ROBBELL
> Let's get comfortable, shall we?

The family sits.

The doctor sits.

> DR. ROBBELL
> Done your deep breathing today?

> FERN
> We didn't know we were supposed to.

Dr. Robbell jumps up.

> DR. ROBBELL
> No wonder you're all so stressed!

He demonstrates and motions for them to stand.

> DR. ROBBELL
> Close off part of your throat. Breathe
> in through your nose, then out
> your nose.

Bert and Fern get up and breathe.

Fern looks at Juice who doesn't buy this. She waves him to comply.

Juice stands and breathes.

All breathe several times.

> DR. ROBBELL
> Feel better? After a little practice
> you'll hear the yogi breath. Then
> you'll be on your way to a state of
> bliss.

Bert and Fern gawk.

Juice gives a jerk-off hand motion.

They all sit.

>   DR. ROBBELL
>   (points to Juice)
>   You're the rotten one,
>   (points to parents)
>   And you're the tortured ones. Right?

>   BERT
>   Dr. Robbell! I don't think you're
>   quite what we had in mind.

Bert stands.

Fern looks up at him quizzically, then stands.

Juice remains seated.

>   DR. ROBBELL
>   Aha! Cognitive dissonance!

>   BERT
>   What?

>   DR. ROBBELL
>   Classical denial.

>   BERT
>   We deny nothing. We came for
>   professional advice and help.

>   DR. ROBBELL

Good.

He motions them to sit.

They sit.

                    DR. ROBBELL
            I understand that you were in a
            terrifying accident in Japan, and
            Juice was left behind to cope on his
            own until his uncle intervened.

                        FERN
            Juice fabricated the whole story.

Dr. Robbell turns to Juice.

                    DR. ROBBELL
            You want your parents dead? Did you
                    hire a hit man?

                        JUICE
            Dude, you've got major brain damage.
                    (to parents)
                Let's get outta here.

Juice stands.

Bert jumps up.

                        BERT
                    Sit down!

                        JUICE

Make me!

Dr. Robbell jumps up. He stretches his arm toward Juice and Bert. His fingers move up and down rapidly.

He makes a twittering noise with his tongue. He gets right up in front of their faces.

They stop, mesmerized.

> DR. ROBBELL
> Sit.

Bert and Juice sit.

The doctor sits. He turns to Fern.

> DR. ROBBELL
> A little something I learned from
> a witch doctor.

Fern glances from Bert to Juice; both are calm.

> DR. ROBBELL
> Now, let's get down to business.

Bert and Juice come out of their daze; they shake their heads.

> BERT
> What was I saying?

> DR. ROBBELL
> I was saying let's get down to business.

BERT
Oh, yes.

Fern gawks at Bert.

DR. ROBBELL
We're going to have to do deep work
here.
(to Juice)
You drop in three times a week after
school.
(to parents)
I'll see you once a week after work,
then all of you come back on Saturday
for a team session.

JUICE
How come I gotta be here so much
and they only gotta be here once?

DR. ROBBELL
They listen. You haven't learned how
to do that yet.

JUICE
Yeah? Up yours.

Juice gets up and slams the door as he leaves.

DR. ROBBELL
We're going to get along just fine.

The doctor nods as he makes eye contact with Bert and Fern.

EXT. PARKING LOT - DAY

Bert and Fern approach their car. They glance around the parking lot and look down the street.

No Juice.

Bert unlocks the car and turns to Fern.

> BERT
> What do we do now?

> FERN
> He's self sufficient. Let's go home.

Bert drives off.

EXT. STREET - DAY

Juice runs down the street after the car, waving his arms.

> JUICE
> Where the hell you going? Hey! Hey!

He stops in the middle of the street, out of breath. He turns around and looks in the direction of Dr. Robbell's office.

INT. DOCTOR'S OFFICE - DAY

Juice enters Dr. Robbell's office.

> DR. ROBBELL
> Ah, you returned to bond into our
> relationship?

> JUICE

They left without me.

DR. ROBBELL
I'm sure it wasn't intentional.
Why don't we take a few minutes to
ease all this stress, then I'll
drop you off at your home.

Juice climbs into the hammock and stares at the ceiling.

The doctor sits cross-legged on top of a large urn half hidden by the foliage.

DR. ROBBELL
I don't care if you utter one
syllable. One of my clients cries
for forty minutes, then apologizes
for the remaining ten. Another client
picks his nose and passes gas because
he was never allowed to do either at
home.
(Beat)
So, if you want to lie in the hammock
and stare at the ceiling for fifty
minutes, that's up to you.

JUICE
I'm not the one sitting on a flower pot.

DR. ROBBELL
I'm not about to fall out of a hammock.

Juice moves a fraction of an inch and tumbles to the floor.

INT. HOUSE - NIGHT

Emily, Fern, and Earl place bowls of food on the table.

Emily goes to the swinging doors.

> EMILY
> Dinner!

O.S. It sounds like a stampede down the stairs.

> BERT (O.S.)
> Slow down.

Kyle and Kimmie burst through the door and scramble to their chairs and sit.

Bert enters the kitchen and kisses Fern on the cheek.

> FERN
> Did you finish your report, dear?

Bert sneaks a piece of lettuce out of the bowl.

Emily whacks his hand.

> BERT
> Ouch! I'll print it later.

The family sits at the table and begins supper.

Juice's place stands out: vacant.

> KIMMIE
> Mommie, where's Kevin?

Fern passes a dish of food to Earl.

All the adults make eye contact.

> FERN
> Giving us a break.

O.S. The front door slams.

The family members make eye contact with each other. A heavy silence fills the room.

The swinging doors slam open as Juice enters.

> EMILY
> Wash your hands, we're just starting
> supper.

She plops a spoonful of potatoes on his dish.

> JUICE
> Why'd you leave me? I had to get a
> ride with that pervert shrink!

> KIMMIE
> What's a pervert, mommie?

> FERN
> A bad man, dear.

> KIMMIE
> Why did you make Kevin go with a bad
> man, mommie?

FERN
We didn't. We'll talk about it later,
okay Kimmie?

Kimmie nods and turns to her dinner plate.

BERT
Were we supposed to search the streets
for you?

JUICE
I was right on the corner!

FERN
Which corner? North, South, East,
or West?

JUICE
I'm not going back to that psychopath!

BERT
He's a little strange but he's one
of the best.

JUICE
Says who? That ding-bat Ms. Morex?

He goes to the sink and washes his hands.

Juice sits down beside Kyle, places his napkin in his lap, piles
food on his plate and scarfs it down.

KYLE

Kevin, can I borrow some of your
comic books?

JUICE
No! And stay out of my room!

Kyle looks disappointed.

The family watch him quietly and nervously as they peck at
their meal.

Juice gets up, slams his chair over and leaves.

EARL
Sometimes he's almost normal.

EMILY
It's like a brain cell gets a flash-
back of his old behavior patterns
or something.

BERT
This plan is not viable.

All nod sadly in agreement.

Music blares overhead.

BERT
What in the world is that?

KYLE
Meat Hook Sodomy.

Fern covers Kimmie's ears.

>   FERN
>   Kyle!

>   KIMMIE
>   That's Cannibal Corpse, Kevin's
>   favorite group when he's not listening
>   to rap.

A creak behind the cafe kitchen doors.

Firework rockets explode into the kitchen and screams around the room.

O.S. Juice laughs.

The family members all scream and run for cover as the room fills with smoke.

The fire alarm blares.

O.S. The front door slams shut, and hysterical laughter fades.

INT. KITCHEN - DAY

The Undertosh's, battle worn, minus Juice, are in a pow-wow around the table.

Fern writes on a ruled tablet.

>   FERN
>   One at a time, please.

>   BERT
>   Mom, you first.

Emily adjusts her glasses and looks at Earl for support.

Earl nods.

> EMILY
>
> Fern, there's too many things going
> through my head. I can't narrow it
> down to one thing.

> EARL
>
> It's okay dear, we're going to make
> a list of everything.

INT. EARL AND EMILY'S BEDROOM - DAY

A large, comfortable room with antique furniture and lots of family pictures and mementos.

> EMILY (O.S.)
>
> There was the time that he nailed
> that insurance advertisement to our
> bedroom wall and spray painted "you're
> old and you're going to die, so do it.
> I could use the room."

Juice spray paints something on the wall, sets the can aside and grabs a piece of paper and a huge nail.

He jams the nail into the wall, through the paper, retrieves the can and exits the room.

BACK TO SCENE

Emily takes a tissue out of her pocket and dabs at her eyes.

EMILY

Our first grandson.

Earl pats her hand.

KYLE

Hey, how about the time when he stuck
all those skewer sticks in my mattress?

INT. KYLE'S ROOM - DAY

Juice strips the sheets and bedspread off Kyle's bed.

He thrusts skewer sticks into the mattress -- pointed end up. He covers the entire mattress.

BACK TO SCENE

Kyle appears upset.

KYLE

He never lets me hang out with him.

Earl looks at Bert.

EARL

How many doors are we up to?

BERT

Oh, I don't know, twelve, I think.

EXT. JUICE'S BEDROOM DOOR - DAY

A whack sound, then a hacksaw blade protrudes from the door. Sawing continues until a huge square falls out of the door.

Bert and Earl run up the stairs.

> BERT
> What's going on here?

Juice sticks his head through the hole.

> JUICE
> I'm making an observation opening.

> EARL
> Ever heard of a dollar ninety-eight
> peephole?

> JUICE
> Never thought of that.

Juice laughs hysterically.

> JUICE
> Oh well.

BACK TO SCENE

Earl shakes his head and points to Fern.

> EARL
> Write that down. A dozen doors,
> holes in the walls, furniture...

> FERN
> Two coffee tables. Actually, three,
> because you fixed the first one twice,

remember?

Bert and Earl nod.

                    KIMMIE
        My Barbie doll, mommie! He pulled
        her hair out and stuck pins in her.

Fern pats Kimmie's hair.

INT. KITCHEN - NIGHT

The family seems burned out.

Several pages list Juice's misdeeds.

                    BERT
              He's got to go.

                    KIMMIE
        Let's nuke his brain in the
        microwave!

Earl makes the thumbs down sign.

Kyle silently runs a finger across his throat.

                    FERN
             It's him or us.

                    EMILY
        Torture the son-of-a-bitch before
        we kill him.

They all have a mad gleam in their eyes.

INT. HARDWARE STORE - DAY

INTERCUT AS NEEDED

Emily pushes a shopping cart. She picks up a box of rat poison, smiles wickedly and puts it in the cart.

Kimmie carries a bar-b-cue basting injector and places it into the cart.

Emily pushes the cart around the corner.

Bert tests the strength of heavy rope. He puts it into the cart and gives the thumbs-up to Emily.

Earl comes down the aisle with some wire. He adds it into the cart.

Fern and Kyle have their arms full of devices.

> BERT
> What in the world are those?

> FERN
> Cattle prods. One for everyone.

She places them into the cart.

END INTERCUT

INT. HOUSE - DAY

The front door opens and the family enters with their purchases.

Juice sits on the sofa in a glazed stupor staring at the TV.

There is no programming, just a blue screen.

> EARL
> (whispers)
> Cellar.

They all tiptoe past Juice.

INT. CELLAR - DAY

Two bare light bulbs with metal deflectors dangle on cords a few feet apart.

Typical cellar with dusty canning jars, a stack of firewood, an abandoned ping-pong table, and a wooden high-backed arm chair.

The family deposits their purchases on the ping-pong table.

Bert and Earl cover the table with an old tarp.

INT. KITCHEN - DAY

The family members eat breakfast.

Juice's chair empty.

An atmosphere of excitement fills the air.

> KIMMIE
> Kevin's still sitting on the sofa,
> mommie.

> FERN
> We know, dear.

> EMILY
> Maybe he's dead. Pray to God for a
> miracle. Maybe we've been spared.

KYLE
Oh Grandma, he's just turbo-blasted.

Everyone stares at Kyle, waiting for a definition.

KYLE
You know, stoned.

EMILY
Oh Lord, new language to learn on
top of all this?

EARL
Every ten years.
We need to get one of those new slang
dictionaries that goes beyond
"groovy."

BERT
Maybe we should check his pulse or
something.

FERN
No, he's just turbo-blasted.

EMILY
Let's check things out.

Emily nods toward the cellar door.

A conspiratorial mood swings among the group.

All get up and go down to the cellar.

INT. LIVING ROOM - DAY

Juice sits on the sofa and stares at the blank TV.

The doorbell rings.

The front door opens after a few moments.

Blowpipe and Edsel enter.

They run up the stairs, then down.

They head toward the living room and spot Juice on the sofa.

> BLOWPIPE
> Hey, dude!

Juice doesn't move.

Blowpipe jumps in front of Juice and waves his arms.

No reaction from Juice.

> EDSEL
> Cool.

He flops down beside Juice and stares at the TV.

Blowpipe joins them.

He changes the channel to "snow," they watch that for a while then turns back to the blue screen.

LATER

Kyle enters the room.

He sits in a chair and looks at the TV.

KYLE
Stupid.

He gets up and leaves.

Earl enters the living room.

He stops dead in his tracks and assesses the boys.

EARL
Nielsons can add a new category to the
rate chart: blue screen.

Juice jumps up and yells.

JUICE
Touchdown! Sold American!
This Bud's for you!

Juice rapidly turns in a tight circle and falls on the coffee table,
which crashes to the floor.

Earl lets out a sigh.

EARL
Four.

Earl exits the room.

INT. UPSTAIRS HALLWAY - NIGHT

Bert, Fern, Earl, and Emily huddle in the hallway. Their eyes
dart to and from Juice's bedroom door.

Juice, Blowpipe, Edsel, and Wormie come up the stairs.

> FERN
>
> Ronnie, how's your mom?

The boys shove past the family and go into Juice's room.

They slam the door.

O.S. The stereo blasts out heavy metal music.

Fern makes an angry face at the door.

> EMILY
> (to Fern)
> Nice try, hon.

> BERT
> He doesn't even remember his name
> is Ronnie, never mind that he
> has a mother.

The sound of walls being body-slammed and head-bashed.

A crash sounds O.S.

Kimmie cries as she runs from her room.

> FERN
> What happened, Kimmie?

> KIMMIE
> Picture fell on my head.

Fern holds Kimmie and kisses her head.

Bert storms into Juice's room.

INT. JUICE'S BEDROOM - DAY

The room is a pigsty with scattered clothes, dirty dishes, blackened banana peels, empty chip bags, and soda cans.

The walls, ceiling and closet door are plastered with hard rock posters and teen paraphernalia.

An iPod stereo sits on a shelf, CD's are scattered all over.

The boys slam-dance.

Bert pulls the stereo plug out of the socket.

The boys dance for a beat longer, then stop, glance around.

Bert points to the door.

                    BERT
                    Leave.

                  BLOWPIPE
                  Bummer.

The boys file out the door.

INT. UPSTAIRS HALLWAY - DAY

Bert and Earl are at the bannister upstairs with a sand-filled punching bag between them.

Fern and Emily stare up at them from the living room downstairs. Bert ties one end of the rope around the bannister.

Earl ties the other end to the punching bag.

Together they lift the bag and toss it over the bannister.

The bannister snaps and the bag and bannister crash below onto the coffee table.

Emily and Fern scream.

                    EARL
                    Five.

INT. DR. ROBBELL'S OFFICE - DAY

Fern and Bert sit on a love seat opposite Dr. Robbell.

All sip coffee from demitasse cups.

Bert and Fern are awkward as they hold the tiny cups.

Dr. Robbell daintily holds the cup with his thumb and index finger, baby finger extended. He sips silently.

His finger becomes lodged in the tiny handle opening. He chuckles as he wrestles with the cup.

Dr. Robbell pulls a tube of K-Y Lubricating Jelly out of his pocket and applies some. He twists the cup.

                DR. ROBBELL
                Must be edema.

                    FERN
                Soap and water?

Dr. Robbell gets up and goes to the bar, turns on the water, gets his hand wet, then pumps the soap container.

He squishes soap on his finger and begins to twist the cup. It gets lodged farther down his finger.

He turns and smiles at the Undertosh's.

DR. ROBBELL
Almost there.

He gives up and smashes it on the counter. The cup shatters.
His finger finally free. He grabs a towel and wipes his hands.

Dr. Robbell returns to his chair and sits.

FERN
What a shame. Is it replaceable?

DR. ROBBELL
No big deal. Fourteenth century,
fifteen hundred bucks a cup.
What the hell.

Bert's cup rattles on the saucer as he sets it down.

Fern pushes her cup and saucer protectively toward the center
of the table.

DR. ROBBELL
Where were we? Oh yes, Fern was saying
that you're formulating a plan?

BERT
We're still working on the details.

DR. ROBBELL
Nonsense. Don't be shy.

FERN

Maybe I was a bit hasty.

Bert nods.

Fern nods.

They get up.

> BERT
> Let us work on it some more and
> then we'll be ready.

Fern nods.

Dr. Robbell gets up.

> DR. ROBBELL
> Leaving so soon?

> FERN
> PTA, we really must rush.

Bert and Fern practically stampede out the door.

INT. LIVING ROOM - DAY

Bert and Fern enter.

There are a couple of thuds from the cellar.

Bert and Fern proceed to the kitchen.

INT. KITCHEN - DAY

Bert opens the cellar door.

> BERT
> Dad?

The thuds are louder.

> EARL (O.S.)
> Son?

Bert and Fern proceed down the stairs.

INT. CELLAR - DAY

Earl, covered with dust, works on the old straight-back chair.

Metal straps are attached to the arms and front rungs of the chair.

A couple of springs from an old sofa stick up from the back of the chair.

Earl holds one end of some wire.

> EARL
> I'm going to splice the wire and
> connect it to the metal.

> BERT
> Will that work?

> EARL
> Hell, I don't know.

> FERN
> At least you're trying.

Fern goes back upstairs.

LATER

Bert, now in jeans and tee-shirt, and Earl check all the spliced connections on the chair.

Earl nods.

> ### EARL
> That'll do.

Bert squats and checks one last spot on the bottom.

> ### BERT
> Let me get this just a little tighter.

Bert stands; he nods to Earl.

> ### EARL
> I'll go get Doll.

Earl walks off to a shadowed corner of the cellar. He returns with an old mannequin, limbs askew, blond hair sticking out all over her head.

> ### BERT
> Does Mom know you're using Doll for this?

Earl plops her down in the chair.

> ### EARL
> This is for a good cause, isn't it?

Bert nods in agreement.

Both are dead serious as they fasten the straps around Doll's limbs.

Earl takes the head wires and fastens them around Doll's head.

> EARL
> Want to do it?

> BERT
> This one's definitely yours.

> EARL
> It is, isn't it?

Earl crosses to the wall and throws a switch.

Electricity buzzes, surges through the chair and mannequin.

The mannequin's sparse clumps of hair go up in a poof of smoke.

EXT. ELECTRIC METER ON HOUSE - DAY

Dial spins.

RETURN TO SCENE

The ceiling bulbs burst.

Sparks fly from the socket, the chair, and the wall switch.

> EARL
> Uh oh.

The cellar plunges into darkness.

EXT. JUNIOR HIGH (MIDDLE) SCHOOL - DAY

The same boys torment Kyle.

Boy #1 grabs Kyle's backpack and tosses it into traffic.

They jostle him as they pass.

Kyle darts between cars to retrieve his battered backpack.

His shoulders slump as he walks home.

INT. KITCHEN - NIGHT

Bert, Fern, Earl and Emily sit around the kitchen table illuminated by candles and drink coffee.

A large bottle of Kahlua sits in the middle of the table.

> FERN
> He was a sweet child.

Everyone nods sadly.

> EARL
> Son, level with me. Did you two
> smoke pot when you were first
> going together?

Bert, Fern and Emily look at Earl as if he's nuts.

> BERT
> Dad, I've never, ever experimented
> with drugs.

> EMILY
> (to Earl)

Are you off your rocker? Maybe they
should have dropped acid.

They sit quietly and think.

> FERN
> I'd give anything just to have him
> appear normal again.

Emily pats Fern's hand.

All nod.

> EARL
> We ought to just capture him and
> change him back.

Bert has a light bulb go off in his head.

> BERT
> What did you say, Dad?

> EARL
> Something silly.

> EMILY
> Something about capturing him.

> FERN
> And changing him back again.

> BERT
> We've got the spare room.

Faces light up.

> ### EARL
> Plan B.

INT. KITCHEN - MORNING

Earl and Emily, in a light mood, wash and dry dishes. You can tell that they like each other's company.

O.S. A dull thud comes from the direction of the living room.

Earl peers at the swinging doors, then back to Emily.

> ### EARL
> Did you hear something?

> ### EMILY
> Thought I did.

The thud sounds again.

Earl puts down the dish towel.

Emily rinses her hands and dries them.

Together they leave the kitchen.

INT. LIVING ROOM - DAY

Earl and Emily stand in the living room and listen, waiting for validation of the noise.

Another thud, comes from outside the front door.

Earl and Emily approach the door; Earl opens it. They peer out.

A blob of grass with dirt attached whizzes past and slams to the floor.

> EARL
> What the hell?

> EMILY
> Now what?

Earl and Emily, shocked, glance from the mess on the floor to the exterior.

They step outside.

EXT. HOUSE - MORNING

Earl and Emily assess their surroundings from the doorway. The door and house are splattered with dirt bombs.

Blowpipe stands in the front yard with a gardening spade. He has gouged the yard around him.

Earl and Emily check out the yard.

Blowpipe's junker car sits at the curb.

> EARL
> Would you mind telling me what this
> is all about?

> BLOWPIPE
> I was trying to hit the doorbell,
> man.

> EARL
> Why didn't you just come up and

ring it?

BLOWPIPE
I was getting close.

EARL
Okay, so your pitching arm is bummed
out; go around to the side of
the house and get the hose
and clean this stuff off.

BLOWPIPE
I don't have time for that now; I've
gotta get Juice. We're going
foraging for mushrooms!

Earl turns to Emily.

EARL
Must have learned a new word.
(to Blowpipe)
Well Blowpipe, you'll have to postpone
your "forage" until this place
is cleaned up.

Juice stumbles through the front door, half-dressed, not quite
awake.

JUICE
Hey dude. What's up?

BLOWPIPE
Gramps is dragging me down.

                    JUICE
                    Bummer.

                    EARL
            Look around. Do other houses have
              dirt all over the doorway?
                    (beat)
            Only ours does. I wonder how this
                   happened?

                    JUICE
             Beats me, I was sleepin'.

He skips down the path to his buddy.

                  BLOWPIPE
            Come on man, let's go!

                    JUICE
                    Where?

                    EMILY
            Foraging. Have a good time. Look
            for the white ones with gilled under-
                     slots.

Emily turns around, goes in the house and slams the door.

                    EARL
            Why aren't you two in school today?

                    JUICE
            Hey, this is a perfectly good day.

Why mess it up with school?

Juice and Blowpipe do the high-five slap and giggle.

> EARL
> Just get out of here.

The boys leave.

> EARL
> Thank God he's not in political
> science.

Earl goes into the house and slams the door.

INT. UPSTAIRS HALLWAY - DAY

Earl measures the spare room doorway.

O.S. the front door opens and close.

> BERT
> Anyone home?

> EARL
> Up here.

Bert climbs the stairs and joins Earl.

> BERT
> It's sure quiet.

> EARL
> The girls went to the store. Kimmie's

at Tammy's house, and Kyle's
sleeping over Jason's.

                    BERT
              Where is he?

                    EARL
              Foraging.

Bert raises his eyebrows.

                    EARL
              Don't ask.

                    BERT
              Let me go change.

Bert leaves.

Earl opens the door and goes inside.

INT. SPARE ROOM - DAY

Earl and Bert stand in the cluttered, unused room.

                    BERT
         I wonder if rebar would be cheaper
              than burglar bars?

                    EARL
         Shoot, that'd be a hassle. Let's
              just measure and have
              something made to fit.

BERT

Better get unbreakable glass for
that window while we're at it.
(Beat)
What about the door?

EARL

We make a facade out of this door
and put up a steel door behind it.
The kind in a nut house with one
of those unbreakable windows.

BERT

That would work.

They move back into the center of the room

EARL

Remove that closet door. Put a
toilet and sink there.

BERT

Let's draw it up.

They nod their heads in agreement and leave.

INT. KITCHEN - DAY

The adults sit at the table.

Earl has a pad of graph paper in front of him with some rough
sketches of the proposed room changes.

The kitchen door bursts open and a filthy, wild-looking Juice
enters, followed by Blowpipe, Edsel, and Wormie.

Wormie clutches a beat up lunch bag.

> EMILY
> I take it you didn't find the white
> gilled ones.

> JUICE
> We looked all over for some, Grandma.

> WORMIE
> Brought you some flat-heads though.

He hands Emily the grungy bag.

> EMILY
> Aren't you sweet to think about me.

She glances at Earl and rolls her eyes.

> FERN
> What in the world were you doing?
> You're filthy and you smell like
> cow poop.

> BLOWPIPE
> I had a hot tip that the pasture was
> booming with 'shrooms, and sure
> enough, those suckers were
> everywhere.

> FERN
> Was this a special project for science
> or something?

The three kids look at each other and shake their heads.

> BERT
> (to Fern)
> Mushrooms, dear.

> FERN
> Oh.
> (looks at boys)
> Don't you realize you could kill
> yourselves eating the wrong ones?

> JUICE
> Chill, mom.

The boys leave.

O.S. they stomp up the stairs.

> WORMIE (O.S.)
> Your mom's into heavy shit, man.

> JUICE (O.S.)
> It's PMS, dude.

The adults look at each other across the table.

> EARL
> Where were we?

Metal music rattles the house.

Bert hastily gets up and leaves the room.

                    BERT (O.S.)
          Kevin! Turn down that stereo before
           I come up there and turn it down
                      myself!

Earl shakes his head, a sad look on his face.

The others appear somber.

The music lowers slightly.

Bert returns to the kitchen and plops down in his chair.

                      EMILY
          Sometimes he seems half-way decent.

The music goes up much louder than before.

All heads turn in the direction of the door.

Everyone scowls.

INT. JUICE'S BEDROOM -- NIGHT

Juice leans against the headboard, zonked out.

Wormie sprawls in a beanbag chair.

Edsel on the bed, crosswise, out cold.

Blowpipe stands on his hands against a wall.

Incense burns on the window sill.

INT. LIVING ROOM - DAY

Emily sits on the sofa looking at a medical book.

A picture of the brain on one page, a surgical procedure on the other page.

Fern enters the room from the front door. She sees Emily and walks over to her and looks over her shoulder.

FERN
Oh, my.

Fern joins her on the sofa.

They both look at the pictures with intense interest.

EMILY
I wonder if we could do that.

FERN
I'd have to be left out of this one.
I can't stand the sight of blood.

Bert comes in. He spots the women and joins them.

BERT
What do you have there?

Emily shows him the open book.

BERT
That'd be a little too gory, don't
you think?

EMILY
That's what we were just discussing.
Oh well, it was a thought. I figured
if we could tweak something in his
brain, maybe we could encourage his

little braincells back to some
semblance of normal.

BERT
Where's dad?

EMILY
He went to the lumber yard and some
salvage place.

A car horn sounds.

BERT
Dad's home.

Car horn blares.

EXT. DRIVEWAY - DAY

Earl's pickup sits in the driveway, loaded: a couple of doors, a
huge, round parking garage-type mirror, and burglar bars.

He gets out of the truck, a big smile on his face.

Bert, Fern and Emily exit the house and join Earl.

EARL
You should have been there son.
What a blast.

BERT
Where in the world did you get all
this?

EARL

Salvage yard East of town. Man,
they've got everything you could
ever want. Cheap, too.

EMILY
You know your father, the ultimate
bargain hunter.

BERT
How much did you spend?

Earl walks to the back of the truck and lowers the tailgate.

He pats a door.

EARL
This door's from the psycho ward
over at the charity hospital.
Twelve bucks.

BERT
You're kidding. That's a two hundred
dollar door.

EARL
Mirror's from the parking garage;
ten bucks.

FERN
Next time I want something, I'm
heading straight for that place.

EMILY

Not without me, you aren't.

Bert takes his jacket off and hands it to Fern.

BERT
Let's get this stuff unloaded before
Kevin gets home.

EMILY
Shouldn't you change first?

BERT
Let's focus on priorities.

The men unload the truck.

The women go back into the house.

INT. DR. ROBBELL'S RECEPTION AREA - DAY

O.S. there's a skirmish.

DR. ROBBELL (O.S.)
What would you like to get off your
chest today?

INT. DR. ROBBELL'S OFFICE - DAY

Dr. Robbell and Juice are in a tangled pile on the floor, rolling, struggling.

RUTH, the receptionist, opens the door and peeks in. She see's the struggle and bursts in the room.

RUTH

Dr. Robbell! Are you okay or should
I call the cops?

Dr. Robbell rolls to the top of the pile and turns to Ruth.

DR. ROBBELL
Everything's under control. Just a
little adjustment to reduce the
dissonance between the affective and
behavioral states.

Ruth appears puzzled.

RUTH
Is it working?

Juice flips Dr. Robbell to the floor with a thud.

DR. ROBBELL
I think so.

JUICE
Dork.

Dr. Robbell thrusts Juice to the floor and jams his arm into his
Adams apple.

Juice gags and struggles.

Ruth looks horrified.

DR. ROBBELL
Everything's under control now, Ruth.

Ruth reluctantly exits.

> DR. ROBBELL
> Where were we? Oh yes, you were
> going to volunteer your innermost
> feelings, the in-equilibrium between
> the cognitive, affective and physical
> aspects of your family unit.
> It's a problem with harmony.

Juice glares up at Dr. Robbell.

Dr. Robbell lifts his arm off Juice's throat, just a pinch.

> DR. ROBBELL
> (sing-song)
> I can't hear you.

> JUICE
> Fuck off, dick-head.

Juice flips the doc to the floor.

EXT. OUTER OFFICE - DAY

Ruth sits at her desk typing.

The outside office door opens and a frumpy MAN and WOMAN enter.

> RUTH
> Mr. and Mrs. Hinkey?

O.S. Yelling and loud thuds come from Dr. Robbell's office.

A picture crashes to the floor.

The Hinkeys look at each other, then back to Ruth.

> RUTH
> Teenager.

They sit down.

> MR. HINKEY
> Oh.

> RUTH
> It won't be long.

Dr. Robbell's office door jerks open and Juice bursts out.

He rushes past Ruth and the Hinkey's and exits, slamming the door in his wake.

Dr. Robbell appears in his doorway, a goofy expression on his face, hair messed up, clothes askew.

> DR. ROBBELL
> (squeaky voice)
> Next.

He ducks back into his office again.

The Hinkeys stare at each other.

INT. LIVING ROOM - DAY

The front door opens and the family enters, wearing their Sunday church clothes.

Kimmie and Kyle dash upstairs.

The adults walk through to the kitchen.

INT. KITCHEN - DAY

Fern walks directly to the coffee pot.

> FERN
> It's coffee.

Emily, Earl and Bert sit at the table.

Fern pours coffee.

O.S. A loud whack disrupts the quiet.

> BERT
> What was that?

O.S. Whack sound again, this time followed by two more whacks, talking and laughing.

> EARL
> We're not going to want to know.

O.S. running down the stairs.

> KIMMIE (O.S.)
> Mommie! All my clothes are on
> the floor.

> FERN
> Now what?

Kimmie enters the kitchen, crying. She runs up to Fern and buries her head in her shoulder.

Fern holds Kimmie.

FERN
Tell Mommie what's wrong.

KIMMIE
(sobbing)
Kevin threw all my clothes on the
floor and took my closet pole.

BERT
What?

Bert and Earl get up and look out the window.

EXT. BACK YARD - DAY

Juice, Edsel, Wormie and Blowpipe are outside, each with a sharpened closet pole that now resembles a giant pencil.

The wooden fence is now gouged with gigantic holes. Some of the boards flop loose.

Kyle stands on the sideline watching.

KYLE
Can I try?

Juice glares at Kyle.

JUICE
Get lost!

Kyle skulks away.

RETURN TO SCENE

> BERT
> My fence!

Fern, Emily, Kimmie, and Earl crowd the window.

Bert storms out the door.

EXT. BACK YARD - DAY

Bert marches across the lawn toward the boys.

A sharpened closet pole whizzes past Bert and strikes the fence.

A look of terror crosses Bert's face.

Bert stomps over to the boys and grabs a pole out of Wormie's hand. He throws it on the ground.

> BERT
> What do you think you're doing?

Earl, Emily and Fern's faces are pressed to the kitchen window.

Blowpipe hurls his pole at the fence and misses. It clears the top and lands in the side of a neighbor's house.

O.S. A NEIGHBOR yells and curses.

The pole whizzes back over the fence to Bert's yard.

> NEIGHBOR (O.S.)
> I'll sue you, Undertosh - you son of a bitch!

Bert groans. He sees all the closet poles on the ground.

BERT
Explain.

JUICE
Practicing for the Olympics.

EDSEL
Yeah, man. We're good at this.

BERT
It's great to have goals, but when
it comes to destroying property, the
plan needs to change.

JUICE
We're not destroying property.

BERT
Look at the fence, Kevin! Can't you
see all the holes? Who's going to
replace the fence boards?
Who's going to pay for all of this?

JUICE
All I'm trying to do is practice so
I can get in the Olympics.

Bert looks from Juice to the boys.

WORMIE
Don't look at me.

                    EDSEL
            He said it was okay.

                  BLOWPIPE
              Not me, man.

                    BERT
        Are these all our closet poles, or
          did you boys bring your own?

                  WORMIE
        Are you kidding? My mom would kill
                    me.

The other two shake their heads "no."

                    BERT
        What made you think you could tear
          our closets apart and use our closet
                  poles?

                    JUICE
              I don't know.

                    BERT
        Find something else to occupy your
        time, like running in front of trains.

                    EDSEL
                  Bummer.

The back door opens and Earl sticks his head out.

> EARL
>
> Javelin catching is the latest craze.

The boys' faces light up. They exit with the poles.

Bert walks to the back door.

> EARL
>
> Teenage shish kabobs.

He gives the thumbs up sign.

INT. SPARE ROOM - DAY

Bert removes the glass from the window.

> BERT
>
> You're sure this glass is unbreakable?

Earl, wearing a tool belt, removes the closet door.

He stops what he's doing, takes the hammer from the tool belt and bashes the unbreakable glass.

> EARL
>
> Yup.

The unbreakable glass leans against the wall, undamaged.

Burglar bars are beside the glass.

EXT. HOUSE - DAY

Bert pushes the lawn mower, and Earl edges.

Kyle picks up twigs.

Blowpipe's car squeals around the corner, crosses the street and screeches to a stop as the front tires jump the curb.

Earl jumps back and falls to the ground.

The car doors open and Juice gets out from behind the wheel.

Blowpipe and Wormie fall out the doors.

Bert and Kyle run up to Earl. They help him up.

> BERT
> Dad! Are you okay?

> KYLE
> You okay, grandpa?

Earl dazedly looks up and shakes his head.

> BERT
> You could have killed your grandfather!
> What were you doing driving?
> You've never had drivers education.
> You don't have a license.

> JUICE
> I did good. I didn't hit Gramps.

> BERT
> You could have made him have a heart
> attack. Look at the lawn.

Juice shrugs.

> JUICE

Gotta keep practicing.

KYLE
Can I learn to drive, dad?

Bert looks at Kyle, aghast.

BERT
You're twelve!

The boys get back in the car.

Kyle runs up to the car.

KYLE
Can I go with you?

JUICE
Go play with Jason!

Juice starts the loud car, puts it in reverse and spins the wheels as he backs up.

Grass and dirt fly everywhere, splattering Bert, Earl and Kyle.

The car squeals down the block and disappears.

EARL
Screw the lawn. Let's get back to
the spare room.

They gather the mower and edger and head for the garage.

Kyle huffs off next door.

INT. SPARE ROOM - DAY

The bars are on the new window, the closet door removed.

Bert and Earl install the new steel door in back of the regular door veneer.

INT. KITCHEN - DAY

The phone rings.

Emily stabs an orange with a hypodermic needle. The box of rat poison sits near a bowl containing a pasty solution.

She grabs the phone.

> EMILY
> Hello?

> DR. ROBBELL (V.O.)
> Is Fern there?

> EMILY
> Yes, wait just a second.

Emily puts the phone down on the counter, goes to the cellar door and opens it.

INT. CELLAR - DAY

Fern stands in the dimly lit cellar, cattle prod in hand.

Doll sits haphazardly in the electric chair.

Fern pokes Doll with the prod.

> FERN
> Take that, you little troublemaker.

EMILY (O.S.)
Fern? Telephone.

Fern jumps from the interruption.

FERN
Be right there.
(to Doll)
Move and you're dead meat.

She leaves the prod in Doll's lap and climbs the stairs to the kitchen.

INT. KITCHEN - DAY

Fern takes the phone.

FERN
Hello?

DR. ROBBELL (V.O.)
Fern? Dr. Robbell. I just wanted to
check and see if everything was okay.
You and Bert missed your session
this week.

FERN
Oh Darn. We've been so busy working
on a special project that it just
slipped our minds. How are your
sessions with Kevin coming along?

INTERCUT - DR. ROBBELL'S OFFICE

Dr. Robbell, in a neck brace, holds the phone and talks.

> DR. ROBBELL
> We're making remarkable progress.

He adjusts the brace.

> DR. ROBBELL
> Is that the plan you mentioned before?

> FERN (V.O.)
> Yes.

> DR. ROBBELL
> How's it coming along?

> FERN (V.O.)
> (whispers)
> Wonderful! I feel like a new person.

Dr. Robbell holds the phone away and look at it quizzically.

> DR. ROBBELL
> Fern, dear, you and Bert wouldn't
> happen to be doing something illegal
> now, would you?

> FERN
> Think of it as pioneering.

> DR. ROBBELL (V.O.)
> Fern, perhaps you and Bert should
> take the time to consider coming in.

Let's sit down and really have a
look at the plan.

FERN
Oh, I don't think Bert would go for
that, Dr. Robbell.

DR. ROBBELL (V.O.)
Well, give it a try and call me back, okay?

FERN
Okay.

She hangs up the phone and faces Emily.

END INTERCUT

EMILY
You going to tell him?

FERN
I don't know. He's a little strange.

Emily stabs the orange again.

INT. DR. ROBBELL'S OFFICE - DAY

Bert and Fern sit across from Dr. Robbell at the desk.

The doctor, in a business suit, appears uncharacteristically
professional.

DR. ROBBELL
I thought it would put you at ease
if I were attired in power clothing

similar to yours, for our patient/
doctor bonding.

BERT
I'd like to get something straight.

DR. ROBBELL
Certainly.

BERT
About this doctor/patient
confidentially thing...

DR. ROBBELL
As far as keeping a secret, I am
a priest.

BERT
No matter what?

DR. ROBBELL
No matter what.

Bert nods, satisfied.

INT. SPARE ROOM - DAY

The spare room now has padded walls, an open bathroom and the garage mirror hanging from the ceiling.

INT. UPSTAIRS HALLWAY - DAY

The spare room door looks just as it did before the renovations.

INT. KITCHEN - DAY

The family, minus Juice, sit around the kitchen table.

An air of excitement is present.

> EARL
>
> Kimmie, you're not going to tell anyone,
> are you?

> KIMMIE
>
> No, Grandpa, I can keep a secret.

> KYLE
>
> Don't worry, Grandpa, we know
> when to zip it.

All gloat.

> BERT
>
> Everyone is concerned because of the
> ruckus this could cause.

> KYLE
>
> Honest, Dad, it's okay. Kimmie and I
> aren't going to squawk.

> KIMMIE
>
> Are we going to have a rehearsal?

> EMILY
>
> No Kimmie, this is a one-shot deal
> and we'd better do it right the first
> time.

O.S. The front door slams.

Everyone makes eye contact with each other.

Kimmie snickers.

Earl holds his finger up to his lips, hushing her.

O.S. several pairs of feet stomp up the stairs.

The stereo blasts.

The family members scramble to the living room.

INT. LIVING ROOM - DAY

The family gets comfortable in front of the TV.

Kyle gets possession of the remote control and flips through channels. They watch a reality show.

                    EARL
        We're pioneers, just like a reality show!

O.S. the stereo shuts off, door slams and several pair of feet stomp down the stairs.

Wormie, Blowpipe, Edsel and Juice parade past the living room and exit the front door.

O.S. Blowpipe's car starts and leaves.

The family members jump up and rush to the door.

The door opens, Juice enters and slams the door shut.

Bert and Earl jump Juice and wrestle him to the floor.

Juice struggles violently.

JUICE
What are you doing? Lemme up.

Juice starts to get the upper hand.

KYLE
Don't let him get away, Dad!

Kimmie screams.

KIMMIE
Do something, Mommie!

Fern darts away and returns with a plastic bat and slams Juice on the back of the head.

Kimmie screams.

Juice slumps.

FERN
I've killed him.

EMILY
That was the plan.

EARL
He's not dead, just passed out.

BERT
Let's get him upstairs before he
comes around.

Bert grabs an arm.

Earl grabs another.

Emily grabs a leg.

Fern grabs the other leg.

> BERT
> The door, Kyle.

Kyle and Kimmie rush ahead of the adults and vault up the stairs.

The foursome proceed with Juice. They stop at the bottom of the stairs and make adjustments.

> EARL
> Everyone ready?

AD LIB confirmations.

They climb the stairs.

INT. HALLWAY - NIGHT

Kyle rushes down the dark hallway to the spare room door. He opens the false door.

INT. SPARE ROOM - NIGHT

At first the dark room appears empty. Then muffled struggles are heard.

Juice, on the floor in a homemade straitjacket and a gag across his mouth, wrestles helplessly.

INT. LIVING ROOM - NIGHT

The doorbell rings.

Fern opens the door to find Edsel in full regalia: black lipstick, eyeliner and shaved eyebrows.

> EDSEL
>
> Hey moms, how's it bouncing? Juice
> around?

Fern opens the door wider and Edsel enters.

> FERN
>
> Hello Theodore. My, don't you look
> interesting tonight. Kevin isn't here.

> EDSEL
>
> Cool, huh? I'm going to meet Lisa
> at the show.

> FERN
>
> Little Lisa Bernstein?

> EDSEL
>
> Yeah, but she's not little anymore.

> FERN
>
> Don't fill me in, Theodore, I don't
> have a strong stomach.

> EDSEL
>
> Where'd Juice go?

> FERN
>
> He didn't say. I assumed he was
> with you, Ronnie or Jeffrey.

> EDSEL
> Gotta go. I'll check him out later.

Edsel approaches the door and opens it.

> FERN
> I'll tell him you stopped by.

Edsel leaves.

Fern closes the door and lets out a sigh of relief.

INT. KITCHEN - NIGHT

Fern returns to the kitchen.

> FERN
> All set. Should we call the cops?

INT. SPARE ROOM -- NIGHT

Juice thrashes around and kicks the floor with his heels. After working up a sweat, he quits.

INT. SPARE ROOM - DAY

Juice sleeps sprawled on the floor. He twitches and slowly wakes up. He tries to stretch and reality returns.

He thrashes about and gives up. Then he rolls and scoots toward the wall and struggles to get himself standing.

Finally, huffing and puffing, he's upright and looks around, wide-eyed.

O.S. a noise at the door.

Juice turns his head quickly to the door window.

A pair of darting eyes peek back at him.

Juice rushes the door, crashes into the pad and bounces off onto the floor. He tumbles over backward onto his back.

He grunts, turns over and gets on his knees and stands.

O.S. Keys jingle; the door opens.

Bert, Fern, Earl and Emily enter.

Kyle and Kimmie peek around the door.

Juice appears furious and rants through the gag and jumps up and down.

Bert grabs him by the shoulders and shakes him soundly.

> BERT
> Shut up and behave yourself.

Juice is shaken like a rag doll.

Bert removes the gag.

> JUICE
> Are you a bunch of lunatics? I'm
> calling the cops! I'm calling Dr.
> Robbell! I'm calling the welfare
> people and have you locked up!

O.S. A toilet flushes.

The spare room door opens and Dr. Robbell enters.

> DR. ROBBELL
> Did I hear my name?

Juice stares wide-eyed.

> FERN
> He wants to call you. Maybe we're
> on the right track.

> DR. ROBBELL
> I knew I made a lasting impression.

> JUICE
> You're a part of this?

> DR. ROBBELL
> It was either join up or be left
> behind, and sonny, no one leaves
> Jonathan Robbell, P-H-D, behind.

Bert and Earl grab Juice's arms, pivot him toward the door.

> JUICE
> Where're we going?

> EARL
> To your fate.

The group proceeds out of the room.

Bert and Earl drag a struggling Juice.

INT. KITCHEN - DAY

The family and the doctor sit along one side of the table, across from Juice, roped into his chair.

EARL

Since I have the most seniority,
I'll do the talking.

Everyone nods agreement.

EARL

A year and a half ago you seem to
have elected yourself to be our
personal representative from Hell.
(Beat)
Son, we took a poll and no one voted
for you, so you're history.

JUICE

You're kicking me out? I'll make
you pay child support.

EARL

Were it that simple, Kevin. If we
kick you out, you'll just find someone
else to make miserable, and we can't
have that over our heads. We decided
you don't deserve to exist anymore.

JUICE

What do you mean?

Fern lunges across the table.

FERN

What your grandfather means is that
we're going to kill you. Have you

got that? Is that clear? D.E.A.D.
The end. Permanent eviction.

Kimmie sticks her tongue out at Juice.

Kyle gives him a smarty-pants look.

Bert gets up and puts an arm around Fern; he guides her back
to her chair.

Fern stews.

> JUICE
> Having a bad day?

> FERN
> You're a bad day. Every day you
> wake is a bad day.

> KIMMIE
> We would have nuked your head
> in the microwave already.

> JUICE
> What kind of shit have you planted
> in her head? What kind of parents
> are you?

> DR. ROBBELL
> Your parents are well-adjusted human
> beings and they've done a fine job
> raising their children, even with
> the way you turned out.

JUICE
Who cares what you think?

DR. ROBBELL
I'm your psychiatrist.

JUICE
You're the one who needs a shrink.
Wait until I get out of here.

Juice jumps around in his chair trying to loosen his bonds.

EMILY
Button your lip and show some respect.

JUICE
Grandma, how can you go along with
this?

EMILY
Having my teeth soaked in Drano and
your Grandfather's hat smeared with
Super Glue did it for me, Kevin.

JUICE
Can't you take a joke?

EARL
You have a dangerous sense of humor,
Kevin.

EMILY
Let's get this ball rolling.

>   (gets up)
>   First, clean him up.

AD lib agreement from everyone as they get up.

Bert begins untying Juice.

Earl joins in, they get Juice free of the chair, stand him up and escort him out of the kitchen.

>   JUICE
>   What's going on? Where're we going?

>   EMILY
>   Bathroom.

>   FERN
>   Project clean-up.

Kyle and Kimmie giggle.

All march up the stairs.

>   JUICE
>   What's with the bathroom?

Emily disappears into the bathroom.

O.S. Water runs in the tub.

Juice stops abruptly; Bert and Earl jerk him along.

>   EARL
>   Don't try my patience, Kevin.

The water sounds louder.

> JUICE
> You're going to drown me?

> EARL
> Durn, we didn't think of that.
> Fern, add that to the list.

INT. BATHROOM - DAY

Bert and Earl enter the bathroom with Juice.

Dr. Robbell, Fern and the kids wait around the doorway in the hall. Emily turns the water off. She joins the others in the hall.

Bert and Earl dump Juice in the tub.

Juice screams at the top of his lungs.

Earl takes the lead, Bert backs off.

Earl dunks Juice's head under water.

Juice comes up sputtering, gasping and coughing.

Earl tries to remove the earring and has a problem.

> EARL
> Fern, could you get this thing out
> of his ear?

> JUICE
> Hey! Leave my earring alone!

Fern enters.

FERN
Oh hush up.

She soundly knocks him on the head.

JUICE
Ow!

Fern removes the earring and returns to the hallway.

Earl grabs the shampoo bottle and pours a dollop onto Juice's hair and begins scrubbing.

JUICE
You're ripping my hair out.

EARL
Rinse.

Before it sinks in, Juice is submerged.

He struggles and comes up sputtering.

EARL
Son, you might want to shut the door
for this next step.

Bert closes the door and returns to the tub.

BERT
Okay Kevin, regular bath time. You
can either do it yourself or we'll
do it for you. Your choice.

JUICE
You're not giving me a bath.

BERT
Well, then, you'd better be a good
boy or daddy and grandpa will show
you the way it should be done.

Bert bends over the tub and unties the straight-jacket arms.

Juice slips out of the jacket.

BERT
You can take your pants off. No tricks.
Remember, you're outnumbered.

JUICE
Do you mind?

EARL
Unless you've got something different,
we're all alike.

JUICE
I'm shy.

Bert and Earl give a look of disbelief and turn their backs.

Juice reluctantly removes his wet clothes and tosses them on
the floor.

EARL
Did you have to do that?

                    JUICE
        I couldn't leave them in here.

                    EARL
                   Why not?

Juice shrugs.

Earl shakes his head.

                    EARL
        See, that's the problem; you don't
        think about anyone else. Are you
            going to clean up the floor?

                    JUICE
                     No.

LATER

Juice sits on the toilet (lid down) a towel wrapped around his waist.

Bert leans against the wall.

Earl sits on the edge of the tub.

A knock on the door.

Bert opens the door and Fern hands him a plastic bag and a pair of hair cutting scissors.

                    JUICE
          What're you going to do??

                    BERT

Your mother wants you to look normal
at the funeral.

Juice jumps up.

JUICE
You're going to cut my hair?

Earl pushes him back on the seat.

EARL
And dye it too.

Juice tries to get up again.

Earl shoves him back down.

JUICE
No way!

BERT
You want the straight-jacket?

Juice grumbles but settles down.

Earl cuts hair. Clumps of hair fall to the floor. The plastic bag falls into the trash can.

The empty dye box follows. Squirting as dye is applied. Water runs.

Hair dryer hums.

Juice stares into the mirror at neatly cut and dyed hair. A good looking normal kid.

                           JUICE
                          Bummer.

Earl appears satisfied.

EXT. HOUSE - DAY

O.S. Tires squeal as Blowpipe's car screeches to a halt. The car doors open and the guys get out.

They go to the front door. Wormie rings the doorbell.

Edsel leans against the door and looks through the peephole. The door opens and Edsel stumbles.

Earl grabs Edsel, preventing him from falling.

                           EARL
              A problem with our equilibrium?

                          EDSEL
             I didn't know you were going to open
                      the door, gramps.

                           EARL
            It's customary to open the door when
               the bell rings, don't you think?

                          EDSEL
                       Oh, yeah, man.

Edsel giggles.

Wormie cuts in front of Edsel.

                         WORMIE

Hey gramps, we're here to get Juice.

                    EARL
          You're too late, he's not here.

                  BLOWPIPE
               Where'd he go?

                    EARL
         He was talking to a girl on the phone
                 and he left.

The guys look at each other in disbelief.

                   EDSEL
                  No way!

                    EARL
        You guys are welcome to hang around
                until he gets back.

                  BLOWPIPE
                 Cool, dude.

They go inside.

INT. HOUSE - DAY

The guys stomp up the stairs to Juice's room.

O.S. the stereo blasts out.

Earl stands at the foot of the stairs and hollers up.

                    EARL

> Turn the stereo down or wait outside.

The stereo lowers.

Bert, Fern and Emily come out of the kitchen and join Earl in the living room.

They all look worried.

BERT
It'll be okay.

Kyle and Kimmie run down the stairs and go outside.

INT. JUICE'S BEDROOM - DAY

The guys make themselves at home, read magazines, listen to the stereo.

INTERCUT TO SPARE ROOM

Juice, in pajamas, slams up against the wall and bounces off.

He looks over the window and burglar bars, approaches the window and grabs hold of the bars and pulls to no avail.

He puts his feet against the wall and yanks, screaming up a storm.

BACK TO SCENE

BLOWPIPE
No sense waiting around here.

They get up.

Wormie shuts off the stereo.

They file out of the room.

INT. LIVING ROOM - DAY

The family members look up as the guys approach the front door.

FERN
Ronnie, tell your mother I said hello.

Wormie grunts.

BLOWPIPE
Moms, we're gonna split.

FERN
Right down the middle?

Edsel laughs.

EDSEL
Split down the middle, get it?

Wormie and Blowpipe give him a bored, exasperated look.

Edsel opens the door and they leave.

O.S. the car starts, backfires, and fades down the street.

INT. SPARE ROOM - NIGHT

Juice sits in a corner.

O.S. Keys jingle.

The door opens and Bert enters carrying a tray of food: meat-loaf, mashed potatoes, peas, milk, bread, Jell-o.

Juice jumps up and rushes past Bert toward the door. He yanks the door open and stops short.

He's face-to-face with Fern.

Fern holds a cattle prod.

She jabs at Juice, makes contact.

Juice screams, jumps back, tumbles to the floor.

> FERN
> Now Kevin, you know better than to
> pull a stunt like that.

Bert stands holding the tray.

> FERN
> Sit down and eat your dinner.

Juice bashes the tray out of Bert's hand and food goes flying.

Mashed potatoes and meatloaf slide down a wall, peas roll across the floor, jello wobbles in a lump on the floor.

One slice of buttered bread slides down the wall and drops off. The milk splatters all over.

> BERT
> You'll feel right at home now.

Bert turns and leaves, taking Fern by the elbow and pivoting her out the door.

O.S. keys turn in the lock. The false door front slams.

Juice stands looking at the mess. He approaches the wall, licks some of the potatoes and meatloaf.

INT. KITCHEN - DAY

The swinging doors slam open and the family tows a struggling Juice into the room.

Bert pushes Juice into a chair.

Earl takes bungee cords and wraps them around Juice and hooks the ends onto the chair rungs.

> EARL
> See, I told you these luggage straps
> would work. No more knots to work
> out of rope.

> BERT
> Good idea, dad.

Emily approaches the kitchen counter where the box of rat poison sits.

She gets a little dish and pours some poison, then adds water. She mixes it with a spoon until she's satisfied.

Next, she opens a drawer and takes out a syringe and loads it up with the solution.

Juice watches full of wide-eyed terror.

> JUICE
> Grandma! Don't you think that's a
> little drastic? When they do
> an autopsy, they'll know someone

killed me.

Emily appears devastated.

> FERN
> We never thought of that now, did
> we?

> EMILY
> I've been practicing for a solid
> week for nothing?

Kimmie enters the kitchen.

> KIMMIE
> Mommie, can I have a cookie?

> FERN
> Of course, dear.

Kimmie goes to the cookie jar and gets a cookie.

> KIMMIE
> Thank you, mommie.

Kimmie kisses Fern on the cheek.

She skips away, out of the kitchen.

Juice sighs with relief.

Emily appears downright depressed.

> EARL

That's okay. We can hang him or use
the electric chair.

All exchange glances of indecision.

                    JUICE
You're never going to get away with
this. My friends'll figure out what's
going on.

                    BERT
Your friends think you ran away from
home and the cops are going to be
very busy questioning them.

                    EARL
The cellar.

Bert nods.

They all get up.

Earl unwraps the bungee cord.

Juice leaps out of the chair and dodges Earl and Bert.

Everyone screams.

Emily and Fern play cat-and-mouse with Juice around the
table.

Juice scoots across the top of the table and slams out of the
swinging doors to the living room.

INT. LIVING ROOM - DAY

The doorbell rings.

Juice bolts to the front door and wrenches it open.

Dr. Robbell stands there smiling.

Emily, Fern, Bert and Earl run into the living room, out of breath.

> EMILY
>
> Don't let him get out!

> DR. ROBBELL
>
> How nice of you to greet me.

Juice screams in horror and takes off running up the stairs.

O.S. A door slams shut.

> DR. ROBBELL
>
> A little family game?

The family runs after Juice, leaving Dr. Robbell at the door.

Emily returns to the door, grabs the doctor by one shoulder and yanks him inside.

> EMILY
>
> Come on!

Dr. Robbell snaps out of his stupor and runs up the stairs.

Emily slams the door, locks it and hurries up the stairs after the doctor.

INT. HALLWAY - DAY

The family members are outside Juice's bedroom.

Fern tries the door.

FERN
Locked!

Dr. Robbell and Emily huff up the stairs and join the group.

DR. ROBBELL
What's going on?

FERN
We were getting ready to kill him and
he escaped.

DR. ROBBELL
Good grief!

BERT
It's a good thing you arrived when you did.

DR. ROBBELL
No kidding.

EMILY
We can't use the rat poison.

DR. ROBBELL
A sure disappointment.

Fern knocks on the door in rapid succession.

FERN
Kevin you come out of that room right

now.

O.S. furniture scrapes the floor.

> JUICE (O.S.)
> This isn't funny mom. You need
> hormones real bad, grandma too.

INT. BEDROOM - DAY

Juice stands in the center of the room looking for an escape route, eyes wide in terror.

> BERT (O.S.)
> Kevin, don't make me break this
> door down.

> EARL (O.S.)
> Why not? We're used to replacing
> doors.

> JUICE
> How about if I go over Wormie's for
> the weekend and give you guys some
> space? Think that'll make you feel
> better?

> FERN (O.S.)
> No deal.

> BERT (O.S.)
> Dad, go get the crowbar. I'm going
> to bash in the door.

INT. HALLWAY - DAY

Earl hurries down the stairs.

> DR. ROBBELL
> We need to have a convergent
> relationship evaluation and validation
> immediately.

All appear puzzled.

Dr. Robbell throws his arms up and yells.

> DR. ROBBELL
> Family session.

> FERN
> We don't have time right now.

> DR. ROBBELL
> Oh yes you do. March, march, march.
> Down those stairs to the kitchen.

Emily looks indignant.

> EMILY
> He'll escape.

> DR. ROBBELL
> Okay. To the living room.
> He'll never get by us. March.

They grumble but march down the stairs, Dr. Robbell pulling up the rear.

INT. LIVING ROOM - DAY

Earl comes through the kitchen swinging doors, crowbar in hand. He joins the others.

> EARL
> Change of plan?

> DR. ROBBELL
> Sanity check.

The family sits on the sofa.

Dr. Robbell stands, arms behind his back.

All eyes are on Dr. Robbell.

> DR. ROBBELL
> Don't you think this has gone far
> enough?

Fern appears shocked.

> FERN
> You approved the plan.

> DR. ROBBELL
> I was under the assumption that you
> were using this tactic to artificially
> exaggerate dissonance, overload with
> dissonance as it were. Kevin would
> then seek equilibrium with a
> behavioral adjustment. It seems that
> the whole family needs it.

> ### EARL
> There's not a jury in this country
> that would convict us. Everyone's
> had at least one teenager.

> ### DR. ROBBELL
> Murder is not the answer.

> ### BERT
> Want him to live with you?

Juice quietly inches down the stairs.

> ### DR. ROBBELL
> Of course not. I'm a bachelor.
> I work long hours. This isn't the
> issue. You cannot murder Kevin.

> ### FERN
> I'll testify against you. You sat
> through the entire planning session
> and agreed with everything.

Juice makes a run for it.

All scream and jump off the couch and charge him.

Juice grabs and yanks the door: locked.

Bert and Earl jump Juice.

Dr. Robbell tries to grab Juice out of their clutches.

> ### EARL
> Let's get to the cellar and get this

over with, once and for all!

They drag Juice with Dr. Robbell in tow down the hall.

INT. KITCHEN - DAY

The family haul Juice to the kitchen then down to the cellar.

> DR. ROBBELL
> You can't do this.

> FERN
> Keep out of this, you quack.

INT. CELLAR - DAY

Bert and Earl slam Juice into the electric chair and strap him down.

Earl slaps duct tape across his mouth.

Dr. Robbell undoes a couple of the straps.

Earl re-straps them.

> EARL
> Don't add to the problem, Doc.

Fern grabs a spray bottle and sprays Juice at the straps.

> BERT
> Good idea. Let's not take any chances.

Dr. Robbell dabs at Juice with a corner of his jacket.

> DR. ROBBELL

Whose idea was this?

EARL
Mine. Pretty good, huh?

Dr. Robbell looks at the chair with respect.

DR. ROBBELL
Primitive but good; of course, this
isn't my area of expertise.

EMILY
Don't be wishy-washy, Doc.

Dr. Robbell appears hurt.

Juice struggles in the chair, wide-eyed. He makes pleading
noises through the tape.

The adults gather around the chair, keyed-up.

Fern gets teary and bawls.

Bert and Emily comfort her.

FERN
My poor little lost lamb.
Where in the world did we go
wrong?

EMILY
Hon, you were a wonderful mother.
He's just a rotten egg.

EARL

Some people slip a disc, you just
had a bad ovary.

DR. ROBBELL
Behavior dysfunction has virtually
no trans-genetic relationship to
the ovaries.

Bert double-checks everything on the chair.

BERT
Okay, we're ready. Who wants the honor?

FERN
I brought him into this world.
It's fitting I take him out.

Everyone nods agreement except the doctor, who looks
defeated.

DR. ROBBELL
I'll lose my license. All those
annuities, my stocks, CD's and no
one to leave them to.

Juice struggles.

EARL
Certificate of deposits or compact discs?

DR. ROBBELL
Both.

Emily gouges him in the ribs.

> EMILY
> Stop whining for Pete's sake. You'll
> go to one of those plush prison's
> anyway. Air hockey in the rec room,
> write your memoirs, putter in the
> garden. You'll even have vegetarian
> and kosher menu choices and a
> wine list.

Juice pops one leg strap. It goes unnoticed.

> BERT
> He's not going anywhere. No one
> will know this is murder, we'll take
> him back upstairs to the bathroom
> and put the radio in the tub with
> him and the cops will think it was
> an accident.

> DR. ROBBELL
> I don't know.

Juice pops the other leg strap, also unnoticed.

> FERN
> Look at all the education you've had
> and you still don't know.

> BERT
> Don't insult the man, hon. He didn't
> study murder 101.

EARL
Yeah, the doc's a good guy.

Juice rolls his eyes and yanks his arms.

The straps pop.

Juice explodes out of the chair and runs up the stairs.

All scream in pursuit.

INT. LIVING ROOM - DAY

Juice unlocks and runs out the front door.

EXT. FRONT YARD - DAY

Dr. Robbell's BMW convertible sits in the driveway with the top down.

The keys dangle in the ignition.

Juice bounds across the lawn and leaps into the car.

He starts the car, throws it in reverse and peels down the driveway.

The car crashes into the huge brick column mailbox.

The family and Dr. Robbell run out the door.

All scream in pursuit.

Juice throws the car into drive and crashes into the steel garage door.

The air bags explode outward. He gets the wind knocked out of him.

EARL

Thirteen -- maybe fourteen.

Dr. Robbell screams upon seeing the car.

DR. ROBBELL
My Beemer!

Dr. Robbell, frenzied, runs to the back of the car, then the front.

Bert and Earl grab Juice and yank him out of the car.

Dr. Robbell runs to Juice and throttles him.

DR. ROBBELL
You irresponsible twit.

Emily and Fern pull Dr. Robbell away.

EARL
Cellar.

All march inside.

Door slams.

INT. CELLAR - DAY

All are gathered around the electric chair.

Juice, bound with rope, and gagged, sits taped and strapped to the chair.

Dr. Robbell sprays water on Juice.

EARL

Places everyone. Fern, you need to
pull that handle down on the wall,
hon.

Fern crosses to the wall and grabs hold of the switch handle. She has a maniacal gleam in her eyes.

EARL
Everybody stand back.

Juice begins to cry.

The family members and Dr. Robbell all have smiles on their faces.

Fern pulls the handle down.

An electrical catastrophe occurs: (FX) lightning, smoke, sparks at the switch only.

An electrical charge races up Fern's arm and envelopes her body.

The charge knocks her off her feet onto the floor.

The lights burst.

FADE TO BLACK

FADE IN:

INT. LIVING ROOM - DAY

Fern lies on the sofa, eyes closed.

Everyone hovers over her, including a bound Juice.

Bert sits beside her on the sofa, patting her hand.

Kimmie cries.

Kyle puts his arm across her shoulder.

> BERT
> Darling... darling, can you hear me?

Fern stirs. Her eyes open wide.

Fern gives one puff and smoke comes out of her mouth. She struggles to sit up.

Bert and Emily prop her up.

She looks at each person, then settles on Juice.

> FERN
> Are we dead?

Juice shakes his head "no" and talks through the gag, not understandable.

> EARL
> A little accident. Thank God you're
> okay.

> BERT
> How do you feel, dear?

> FERN
> Add salt.

Fern plops back down on her back.

> EMILY

Now what?

EARL
(to Juice)
You get upstairs to the spare room
and be good or I'll plunk your butt
back in that chair.

Juice charges up the stairs.

BERT
I'd better go untie him and lock
the door.

DR. ROBBELL
I'll go. You stay with Fern.

EARL
Make sure you lock the door after him, Doc.

DR. ROBBELL
I promise.

Dr. Robbell takes off after Juice.

The doorbell rings.

Emily approaches the door and looks through the peephole.
Officer Lajoda and officer #1 stand at the door.

Emily turns around, stricken.

EMILY
Cops!

BERT
We reported him missing.

Emily lets out a sigh, pats her hair, adjusts her facial expression, and opens the door.

EMILY
Hello, officers. Won't you come in?

OFFICER LAJODA
Are you the party that reported a
missing child?

EMILY
My daughter-in-law called; my grandson
is missing.

Officer Lajoda and Officer #1 enter.

Bert comes forward.

OFFICER LAJODA
When was the last time you saw your
son?

Fern struggles to sit up on the sofa.

EMILY
This has just floored my daughter-
in-law.

The officers shake their heads, sadly.

FERN
Yesterday afternoon. His friends
dropped him off, he ran upstairs
then he left again.

OFFICER #1
Did he leave alone or with his
buddies?

BERT
Alone. A couple of his friends came
back later looking for him.

EARL
He never stays away without letting
us know where he is. Something's
not right.

Dr. Robbell comes down the stairs. He introduces himself to
the police and hands each his business card.

DR. ROBBELL
Jonathan Robbell, the boy's
psychiatrist.

OFFICER LAJODA
Was he seeing you regularly?

DR. ROBBELL
Yes. Psycho-sociopathic tendencies
with obvious and concomitant anti-
social behavioral consequences.

OFFICER #1
Think he could be a runaway?

DR. ROBBELL
No doubt about it. Psychotic episodes
frequently manifest within the context
of psychopathology. Why, he may even
believe that someone is trying to
kill him.

The cops shake their heads, knowingly.

OFFICER LAJODA
We'll list him as a runaway. If he
should contact you, let us know.

The doorbell rings.

Earl goes to the door and opens it.

Wormie, Blowpipe and Edsel are there; they come in.

WORMIE
Wow, cops! Can I see your gun, dude?

Officer #1 puts his hand protectively on his gun.

Officer Lajoda turns to Bert.

OFFICER LAJODA
These the friends you mentioned?

BERT
Kevin's best friends.

EARL
They're inseparable.

OFFICER LAJODA
Okay boys, let's go for a walk
outside.
(to family)
We'll take care of everything.

The cops and the boys leave.

The family members let out a sigh of relief.

Dr. Robbell hyperventilates.

Earl pounds him on the back.

BERT
Don't do that, dad. Get a paper
bag.

Earl rushes to the kitchen and returns with a paper lunch sack, shakes it open and shoves it at Dr. Robbell.

BERT
Okay Jonathan, just breathe, in and
out. In and out.

Dr. Robbell follows instructions and calms down.

DR. ROBBELL
Red line overload. Warning. Losing
it results in electroshock convulsive
therapy.

(beat)
I can be kind to myself.

BERT
Everyone's excited.

Fern gets up off the sofa, wobbly.

Pieces of her sleeves and slacks fall off.

FERN
We're failures.

DR. ROBBELL
No, you're trying to move too fast.

EMILY
Yup, slow down and think things out.

DR. ROBBELL
Exactly.

EARL
We still have a few options left.

INT. ATTIC - NIGHT

Bert bolts something to the rafters.

INT. LIVING ROOM - NIGHT

Emily and Fern look up to the ceiling.

Earl and Dr. Robbell are on the upstairs landing looking across
to the chandelier.

The chandelier shows a meat hook close to the base.

Attic stairs are folded down in the upstairs hallway.

Bert emerges from the attic, down the stairs.

He folds the stairs and closes the opening.

He joins Earl and Dr. Robbell.

                    BERT
            Oh yeah, that'll work.

Earl stoops and picks up a long snare pole with rope attached.
The other end of the rope sports a hangman's noose.

                    EARL
        Now let's see how good the old
              coordination is.

Earl eases the pole over the balcony, the rope trailing behind.

He leans forward and stretches out, trying to hook the rope over
the meat hook.

                    BERT
              Careful, Dad.

                    EARL
        Don't you worry, your old dad can
              take care of himself.

                    EMILY
        For heavens sake Earl, who do you
        think you are, Indiana Jones? Let

Bert take care of that.

EARL
I'm not totally worn out, Emily.
There are things I can do besides
the dishes.

EMILY
Your father's gone off the deep end.

BERT
Mom, he's fine.

All eyes watch as Earl snares the rope to the hook.

Fern and Emily clap.

LATER

Emily, Earl, Dr. Robbell, Bert stand on the landing.

Juice, with the rope around his neck, peers over the railing.

BERT
Everyone ready?

JUICE
I'm not ready.

FERN
Wait just a sec.

Fern pulls the coffee table out of the way.

EARL

Good idea.

FERN

Don't want to take any chances.

Emily stands in front of the coffee table and looks up at the hook, judging.

EMILY

You're clear.

JUICE

I'm not ready.

BERT

Since when do you pay attention to
what anyone says?

JUICE

Since right now.

EARL

Should have thought of that a long
time ago.

BERT

Okay, now get up there and jump.

JUICE

Are you crazy?

The whole situation from Juice's P.O.V.: bannister, hook, rope, the long way down to Fern and Emily.

EARL
You want something done, best do it
yourself.

Bert nods agreement.

Bert and Earl grab Juice, catching him off guard and pitch him over the railing.

Juice screams.

The rope swings wide and slips off the hook.

Juice flies through the air and crash lands on Fern - and the coffee table.

BERT
Holy cow.

Everyone dashes down the stairs.

Bert and Earl grab Juice and haul him off Fern, placing him on the carpet, face up.

His eyes stare blankly.

Fern is spread-eagle on the collapsed coffee table, a frozen look of terror on her face.

EMILY
Are they dead?

Bert, Earl and Emily hover over Fern.

Dr. Robbell pushes his way through to Fern's side and squats beside her.

He holds her wrist, taking her pulse.

DR. ROBBELL
She's fine.

He gets up and goes over to Juice and takes his pulse.

DR. ROBBELL
He's fine. Everyone's fine.

Fern's eyes blink.

EMILY
She's coming around.
(to Fern)
Are you okay?

Fern struggles to sit up.

Bert helps her.

FERN
I saw this bright light, sparkly
clouds with angels... I know I was
in heaven.
(beat)
We have to paint the living room
gold! An orange sun over the
fireplace!

EMILY
Hon, it was just the chandelier.

Emily points up; the light blazes.

> FERN
> Oh.

Earl stares at the smashed coffee table.

> EARL
> Six.

INT. KITCHEN - DAY

Fern and Bert wear business suits. They check their brief-cases.

Earl and Emily prepare lunch sacks.

Kimmie and Kyle dash through the swinging doors, grab their lunch bags and kiss their mother and grandmother.

Kimmie kisses the men.

> KYLE
> Bye, Dad. Bye, Grandpa.

> BERT
> Have a good day at school.

The kids exit through the swinging doors. O.S. the front door slams.

The phone rings.

Fern answers it.

Emily prepares a tray of food.

FERN
Hello?

MS MOREX (V.O.)
Mrs. Undertosh? Ms. Morex here.

FERN
Good morning, Ms. Morex, how are
you?

Fern and Emily make eye contact.

The men put the paper aside and listen.

MS MOREX (V.O.)
I'm fine. How are you? I'm sorry
to hear about Kevin. Has there been
any word?

Fern gives the okay signal with thumb and index finger.

FERN
I'm afraid not.
No one's heard a word from him.
We're praying he's not dead somewhere.

MS MOREX (V.O.)
He's merely confused. I'm sure he'll
show up soon.

FERN
Thanks.

Fern hangs up.

Everyone goes back to what they were doing.

EMILY
Who wants the honor?

She holds the tray of breakfast food.

FERN
I'll go.

INT. HALLWAY - DAY

Fern unlocks the door on the spare room and enters.

INT. SPARE ROOM - DAY

Juice sleeps on the floor, wrapped in a blanket.

FERN
Rise and shine, Kevin.

Juice stirs, wakes.

FERN
Good morning.

JUICE
Morning, Mom.

Fern raises her eyebrows.

FERN
Grandma made you a wonderful

breakfast.

Juice sits.

Fern places the tray on his lap.

> JUICE
> Wow, this looks great.

He digs into the muffin and juice.

> JUICE
> Hey, this isn't poisoned, is it?

> FERN
> Of course not, silly. I'm off to
> work.

> JUICE
> Hey Mom, can you bring me a couple
> of magazines or something?

> FERN
> Which ones do you want?

> JUICE
> National Geographics.

> FERN
> (surprised)
> We just received the new issue
> yesterday. I'll go get it.

JUICE
Thanks, Mom.

Juice resumes eating as Fern exits the room.

EXT. SIDEWALK - DAY

Kyle walks home from school.

The four gang members surround Kyle. They push and shove him relentlessly.

INT. SPARE ROOM - AFTERNOON

Juice and Kyle sit on the floor and play checkers.

JUICE
King me.

KYLE
That was just luck.

Juice ruffles Kyle's hair.

INT. LIVING ROOM - NIGHT

The doorbell rings.

Bert comes through the kitchen doors and answers the front door.

Two middle-aged couples, GARY, VICKI, JIMMY, and DIANA stand on the doorstep.

Fern comes through the kitchen and joins Bert.

BERT
Well I'll be.

(shakes hands)
Haven't seen you in ages.

FERN
Come in. Come in.

The two couples enter the house.

Bert closes the door.

Fern and each lady hug.

FERN
Vicki, I didn't see you at the PTA
meeting.

VICKI
Couldn't get off work in time.

GARY
We wanted to give you our support
over this thing with Juice...
I mean Kevin.

Emily and Earl come out of the kitchen. They all sit in the living room.

Emily returns to kitchen.

EARL
Hi Jimmy. Saw you at the grocery
store when we were leaving yesterday.

BERT

It was very difficult the first few days,
but we've adjusted.

Bert, Fern and Earl look real serious.

The visiters return sympathetic looks.

VICKI
The boys are down-right despondent.

JIMMY
Ronnie hasn't been concentrating on
his school work lately.

Emily brings out a tray loaded with coffee items.

DIANA
We should be doing this for you. How
you've suffered these past few weeks.

Earl can't believe what he's hearing.

EARL
Vicki, Gary David, I've known you
all your lives. Your folks and I
went to school together. Same with
you two.
(nods to Jimmy and Diana)
Let's face facts here. These past
couple of weeks have been the first
peace and quiet we've had in months.

The two couples appear shocked.

VICKI
Mr. Undertosh?

EARL
It's the truth.

FERN
Diana, how many times have you called
me crying your eyes out because of
some dimwitted thing Theodore did?

Diana squirms under fire.

DIANA
There may have been a few times...

BERT
Nonsense. Our sons have turned into
nightmares. They've cost us money
in repairs, legal fees, psychiatrist
bills. I can't even add everything
unless I have a ledger and a
calculator.

JIMMY
You're just strung out with this
run-away business.

EMILY
(to Jimmy)
Your mother would wash your mouth
out with soap if she heard you.
These boys are monsters. Face facts

and deal with the real world.

> BERT
> What would you pay for peace and
> quiet if you could?

> GARY
> What do you mean?

> BERT
> Follow, please.

INT. HALLWAY - NIGHT

The group stands in front of the spare room door.

Bert opens the spare door facade.

The visitors gaze at each other in amazement.

Bert invites each of them to peer through the window into the room.

After both couples look, Bert quietly closes the spare door facade and they all tip-toe down the hallway and stairs.

> GARY
> Vicki, we've got work to do.

> DIANA
> Jimmy, get the coats. We need to
> get a good night's sleep before we
> go to the bank and take out a loan.

> VICKI

> (to Fern and Emily)
> He must have been a handful.

FERN
Straitjacket.

Emily hurries out of the room and returns with a spare jacket.

All women look as Emily points.

EMILY
Flat felt seams.

FERN
They won't come apart.

JIMMY
(to Earl and Bert)
Where'd you get that padding?

EARL
Salvage yard.

BERT
East of town.

Jimmy, Diana, Gary, and Vicki rush out the door, excited.

INT. BEDROOM - DAY

Juice, dressed in jeans and t-shirt, cleans his old bedroom.

He tosses candy wrappers, banana peels and trash into a garbage bag.

An easy listening song plays softly.

The front door slams O.S. and feet run up the stairs.

A door slams.

Juice sticks his head out of his room and looks down the hall.

Kyle's door is closed.

He goes to Kyle's door. He hears crying. He knocks.

> KYLE (O.S.)
> Go away!

Juice opens his door and enters.

Kyle lies on his stomach his head buried into his pillow.

> JUICE
> What's wrong?

He turns Kyle over.

Kyle has a bruise under his eye.

> JUICE
> Who did this to you?

> KYLE
> These four gang members keep picking
> on me. They won't leave me alone.

> JUICE
> Where do they hang out?

KYLE
They bully kids at the park.

JUICE
Nobody picks on my little brother!

Juice gets up and goes to his room, Kyle on his heels.

He tears off his shirt and puts on one of his graffiti shirts.

He looks in the mirror and messes up his hair. He pulls a bottle of colored hair spray out of the trash and sprays his hair.

Juice grabs his phone and makes a call.

JUICE
Hey, I need some help. Yeah, I'm
back home. Come pick me and Kyle
up.

Fern comes into the room. She stares in shock at Juice.

FERN
Kevin!

Then she see's Kyle's bruise.

FERN
Kyle, what happened?

JUICE
It's okay mom. The boys are picking
us up and I'm going to make sure no
one bothers Kyle again.

Juice kisses Fern on the cheek.

O.S. Blowpipe's car pulls up to the house.

Juice and Kyle exit the room.

> JUICE
> Gotta go, mom. We'll be right back,
> I promise.

Fern is right on their heels.

Juice and Kyle hurry down the stairs.

Emily and Earl come into the living room as the boys go out the door.

EXT. PARK - DAY

The four gang members hang out and talk on their cell phones.

Blowpipe's junker car pulls up to the curb and they all get out, including Kyle.

> BOY #1
> Well, if it isn't the freaks.

The gang member looks at Kyle.

> BOY #1
> Are they going to protect you?

Kyle looks scared.

> JUICE
> Kyle, go back to the car.

Kyle hurries back to the car, gets inside and locks the door.

JUICE
You need a belt for those pants, dude?

Blowpipe, Wormie and Edsel laugh crazily.

WORMIE
You look like you got a load in your pants.

BLOWPIPE
Yeah, go over to the bathroom and
take a dump, will you?

BOY #2
At least we're not freaks like you.

Juice gets in the gang member's face (Boy #1)

JUICE
Nobody beats up on my little brother.

BOY #1
Aaahhh, how sentimental. What're you
going to do about it?

They all commence fighting.

JUICE
Head-bashing time, dudes!

Juice, Blowpipe, Wormie and Edsel bash their heads against the
gang members heads.

The gang members grab their bruised heads and groan in pain.

JUICE
Don't you ever bother my brother
again, you understand?

The gang members hobble down the sidewalk.

Kyle gets out of the car, excited.

KYLE
Wow! That was awesome!

WORMIE
Those fu...

Juice slaps his hand over Wormie's mouth.

JUICE
No cussing. It'll imprint on his
brain!

Wormie's eyes open wide.

WORMIE
Oh, yeah. Sorry, dude.

INT. JUICE'S BEDROOM - DAY

Juice is changed into nice clothes and his hair is neat and clean.

He finds a dart and tosses it at the target on the wall and makes a bull's-eye.

Next, he sorts through clothes scattered around, making two piles: loud, flashy graffiti clothes are the biggest pile.

He digs through the trash bag retrieving the magazines and stacks them on the clothes.

He goes to the stereo and begins tossing tapes and CD's onto the pile and straightens out the remaining few.

LATER

The spotless bedroom holds a neat pile of discards by the open door.

Mozart, Einstein and Shakespeare posters hang on the walls.

Juice sits on the bed looking at an encyclopedia volume.

Fern knocks on the door frame.

Juice turns to her.

JUICE

Hi, mom. Come on in.

Fern crosses the room and sits on the bed with Juice.

FERN

Are you going to tell me what happened?

JUICE

These bad kids were trying to get
Kyle to join their gang.

Fern hugs Juice.

FERN

I'm proud of you.
(beat)
Your room looks wonderful, Kevin.

JUICE
Thanks, Mom. Can we bring my old
stuff to the trade shop in town?

FERN
Of course, dear.

She looks over to the stack of clothing.

FERN
Looks like we need to do a little
clothes shopping.

JUICE
I won't need much since school's out
next month. I'm going to get a job
so I can save up for a car.

FERN
Splendid. I'm sure your father and
grandfather can help you pick out
the best bargain.

JUICE
Yeah, grandpa knows cars inside and
out.

Fern gets up to leave.

Juice stands and hugs her.

> JUICE
> Thanks for everything, Mom.

> FERN
> Welcome back, Kevin. I've missed you.

INT. HIGH SCHOOL - DAY

Students traverse the corridors.

They stare and whisper as Juice opens his locker.

He closes his locker, turns to leave and bumps into Brenda.

> JUICE
> Oh hi, Brenda. Sorry, I didn't see
> you.

Brenda leans up against the lockers, looking shy.

> BRENDA
> I like your new look, Kevin.

> JUICE
> I got tired of looking like a slob.
> (beat)
> What are you going to do when school's
> out?

> BRENDA
> I've got a part-time job at Pizza
> Monster, and I'll be baby sitting off

and on. You?

They walk down the corridor together.

> JUICE
> A full-time job. We'll be seniors
> next year and I want to save for
> college.

> BRENDA
> I didn't know you were going to go
> to college.

> JUICE
> Gosh, yes. You can't get anywhere
> without a college degree these days.

> BRENDA
> Sounds like you're going to be real
> busy this summer.

> JUICE
> I won't be that busy. Maybe we could
> go to a movie sometime.

> BRENDA
> Love to. Here, let me give you my
> phone number.

Brenda opens a notebook, writes her name and number down
and tears it off and hands it to him.

Juice smiles widely.

Bell rings.

JUICE
I'll call you.

They rush off in separate directions.

EXT. HOUSE - DAY

Juice rides Kimmie on his bike down the sidewalk, balancing her on the handlebars.

A police car pulls up to the curb and stops.

Officer Lajoda gets out and approaches Juice.

Juice stops the bike.

Kimmie jumps off.

OFFICER LAJODA
Kevin Undertosh?

JUICE
Yes, sir.

Kimmie runs to the house and enters.

OFFICER LAJODA
I need to ask you a few questions
about Theodore Shoemaker and Ronald
Bigan.

JUICE
What about them? We haven't hung out
together for a couple of months.

The front door opens and Emily, Earl and Kimmie come outside and join Juice.

EARL
Problem, officer?

OFFICER LAJODA
Trying to track down a couple of run-aways.

JUICE
Wormie and Edsel.

EARL
They haven't been around since before school let out.
(to Juice)
Did you talk to them at school?

JUICE
No Grandpa.
(to Officer Lajoda)
Wish I could tell you something but I don't know where they are. Have you checked with Blowpipe? His real name is Jeffrey.

OFFICER LAJODA
I just came from his place. He's upset because they didn't take him with them.

EMILY

Lord, what next?

                    EARL
        I'm sure they'll miss three meals
                a day soon.

Officer Lajoda gets in his car and leaves.

Emily, Earl, Kimmie and Juice eye each other knowingly.

INT. KITCHEN - DAY

Emily and Fern busily prepare dinner.

Kimmie sets the table.

O.S. The doorbell rings.

Bert answers the door.

Dr. Robbell, dressed in casual clothes, enters.

                 DR. ROBBELL
              Hope I'm not late.

                    BERT
                Right on time.

Earl gets up and shakes hands with the doctor.

                    EARL
            Doc. How's it going?

                 DR. ROBBELL
          Business is booming. It's a sick
                  society.

Earl grunts.

Emily sticks her head into the room.

> ### EMILY
> Dinner's ready.

The men get up and proceed into the kitchen.

Kyle thunders down the stairs.

> ### BERT
> Hold on there young man, you'll wear out those stairs.

> ### KYLE
> Sorry, Dad.

INT. KITCHEN - DAY

Everyone sits down.

Juice's chair is empty.

> ### DR. ROBBELL
> Where's Kevin?

> ### FERN
> He should be here soon, he went to
> the movies with Brenda.

As the serving bowls are passed:

> ### DR. ROBBELL
> Has he got a counter-gender repository
> for his hormone-slated juxtaposition

in his generational constellation?

All eyes are on Dr. Robbell.

> EARL
> Can we have that in English, doc?

> DR. ROBBELL
> He has a girlfriend?

> EMILY
> A pretty little thing, so sweet.

O.S. the front door opens and closes.

> FERN
> That must be him now.

The swinging doors open and Juice enters followed by GORDON, 16, dressed to the max in tie-dyed clothes, leather vest, dangling chains.

> JUICE
> Sorry I'm late. I brought Gordon
> home for dinner. I hope there's
> enough.

All stare at the boy.

> BERT
> There's plenty.

Emily gets up and gets dishes and silverware.

JUICE
This is Gordon, but you can call him
Stinkbomb. He doesn't have anywhere
else to go and I thought maybe we
could help him out.

Emily puts the place setting on the table beside Juice's place.

Juice grabs an extra chair and the boys sit down.

STINKBOMB
Wow, this is really great.

FERN
Do your parents know where you are?

The serving bowls are passed around.

STINKBOMB
They don't care. They kicked me
out.

The family members have a dangerous gleam in their
eyes.

Dr. Robbell takes it all in quietly.

FERN
We have a spare room and you're more
than welcome to stay.

All appear very welcoming.

Dr. Robbell looks alarmed.

STINKBOMB
Wow, that's great.
(to Juice)
Your folks are real cool.

Emily gets up and goes to the counter.

She mixes a glass of instant lemonade and sets it down in front of Stinkbomb.

Dr. Robbell glances over to the counter and see's the box of rat poison.

He lunges across the table, grabbing the glass out of Stinkbomb's hand. He raises it to his eyes.

STINKBOMB
Hey!

DR. ROBBELL
Look at that dirty glass! Let me
get you another one.

Dr. Robbell glares at Emily.

She looks disappointed.

Dr. Robbell gets up, rinses the glass, gets a clean one, fixes the drink and gives it to Stinkbomb.

DR. ROBBELL
Emergency family meeting. Chop chop.
Adults only.

The adults grumble, but get up and march into the living room.

Kimmie and Kyle giggle.

Juice nudges Stinkbomb.

> JUICE
> They do this all the time.

The kids continue to eat.

> DR. ROBBELL (O.S.)
> First, everyone, breathe...

> EARL (O.S.)
> Doc... Doc you could go on the speaker
> circuit.

> FERN (O.S.)
> Write a book.

O.S. Hyperventilation.

> EMILY (O.S.)
> Talk shows.

> BERT (O.S.)
> Calm down, Jonathan. Dad, grab that paper sack...

FADE OUT.

ABOUT THE AUTHOR

Dawn Greenfield Ireland, also known as D.E. Greenfield & DG Ireland, is an award-winning author of 22 novels, (5 series: cozy mystery, sci fi/fantasy, billionaire shapeshifters, and dystopian), and a stand-alone sci-fi romantic adventure.

Most of her 7 nonfiction books have won awards. Dawn has adapted a few of her award-winning screenplays into book format, and several of her books into TV series format. She also created over 50 themed notebooks.

She had two screenplays optioned, and she worked on a screen-writer-for-hire project. Dawn has a certificate from the Professional Program in Screenwriting from UCLA (2002), and a certificate from ScreenwritingU (2023).

Dawn writes full-time. She lives among dreams and fantasies with two cats and moving boxes. Her head is filled with stories. She doesn't suffer from writer's block. Every word she has written and published is from her noggin (brain, in case you don't know what noggin means). Her fiction is all make-believe from the deep dive into her imagination. Her nonfiction has been researched until her brain has numbed.

Dawn's business, Artistic Origins, has been around since 1995. Besides writing, she coaches writers, edits, formats, and publishes clients' books. Her former day job as an award-winning technical writer played a major role in her fiction writing. She is detailed-oriented, the organizational queen of the known universe, and never misses a deadline.

www.degreenfield.com

 facebook.com/dawn.ireland.18

x.com/dawnireland

 instagram.com/dawngreenfieldIreland

 goodreads.com/dawnireland

 linkedin.com/dawnireland